'Sandy

Operation Sandy

Cathie Bartlam

Scripture Union
130 City Road, London EC1V 2NJ

By the same author:
Go for Gold

First published 1989

ISBN 0 86201 551 0

Phototypeset by Input Typesetting Ltd, London
Printed and bound in Great Britain by Cox and Wyman Ltd, Reading.

1

The moment Mick saw Sandy he knew that one day she would be his. Her damp, dark eyes gazed up at him without blinking. The loose folds of skin on her tiny head wrinkled above her eyebrows, giving her a puzzled expression. She seemed to be wondering whether he was friend or foe.

'Hello, little pup,' Mick whispered. 'You're beautiful.' Carefully he reached out just two fingers and softly stroked the velvet head. 'You're going to be mine. I know it.'

'Hey, come on. Shift out of the way. She's our pup, you know,' John barged past Mick almost knocking him over.

'I'm only looking,' protested Mick.

'Well, you just budge and let me have a good look. Move!'

John's mum came running down the stairs. 'Just leave the little thing alone. You'll frighten her with all that noise.'

I won't frighten her, thought Mick. Big, clumsy, loud-mouthed John will, but I won't. She's going to love me much more than him.

With all the commotion, Sandy started to whine. She was only six weeks old and missed her mother.

'Now look what you've done,' scolded John's mum. 'She had only just gone off to sleep.'

Mrs Greer scooped up the pup, who immediately wee-ed all down the front of her jumper. John and Mick forgot their rivalry, as they started to laugh. Mrs Greer wasn't amused.

'If I were you,' she said slowly through clenched teeth, 'I would make myself scarce. This is the third jumper she's wet so far today and I've just about had enough. Get yourselves a snack. I don't want to so much as hear you until Mick's mum comes.'

The boys calmed down at once. They knew when Mrs Greer was being serious.

'Let's make a space sandwich,' said John.

'Okay,' agreed Mick. 'It's my turn to choose. I want green asteroids.'

'I can't find anything green,' said John, rummaging in the cupboard, 'only something called dried peppers.'

'They'll do ,' said Mick. He had covered two slices of bread with peanut butter and cheese. John sprinkled on the peppers and the boys took their sandwiches outside.

They were revolting, so they had a competition to see who could flick bits of green pepper the farthest. John won as usual. He was a big strong boy with lots of blond hair and deep blue eyes that sparkled when he was excited. Most of the time he looked as if he was growing out of his clothes, which clung tightly to his broad body. By contrast Mick was small and thin, with brown hair that stuck up all over the place. His face was pale and most of the time his green eyes were serious.

It was strange that he and Mick were such good friends as they were so different. Mick was a fast runner who seemed to pop up suddenly and quietly in all sorts of places. John, however, lumbered around, barging into people and talking in a loud voice. He loved competitions and Mick often invented games for them to play.

'Let's play "Treasure",' Mick suggested. 'We have half an hour to collect as many weird things as possible that will fit into a cup. Okay?'

'Great,' said John, disappearing eagerly to hunt for weird things. Mick shoved a few pebbles and leaves into a pile, so it looked as if he had done something. Then he curled up by the big bush at the bottom of the garden, in his favourite thinking position. He had to work out how to get Sandy to be his own. The problem was going to be hard to solve. You see, not only did the pup live here with John's family, she did not even belong here. Mrs Greer, John's mum, had been telling them about it for weeks.

He tried to remember what she had said. Bits came back to him . . . 'of course, the Guide Dog people will keep an eye on her . . . it's called puppy walking . . . when she's ten months old she goes back to them for training . . . then we will have another one.'

Mick sat up with a start! The Guide Dog people could do what they liked with other pups but not with Sandy! There was no way she was going back to them, for training or anything else. Not only had he got to get her off John's family but off these mysterious Guide Dog people as well. However could he do it?

'I've got millions!' John's voice broke through the silence. 'Bet I've won.'

Mick jumped to his feet, brushing dead leaves off his clothes. He did not want John to know about his plans for Sandy.

'Come on!' yelled John. 'Where's your measly pile of treasure?'

Mick pointed half-heartedly at his little heap, as John emptied out a bucket full of things onto the grass.

They were still arguing about who was going to return the brass door knocker to next-door's house when Mrs Greer appeared.

'Your mum's just coming, Mick,' she said. 'Go and have a quick wash. You look like you have been in a bush!'

I have, thought Mick. He wished Mrs Greer would not make such a fuss about him being clean when Mum arrived. His mum did not seem to notice what he looked like.

'Can I see Sandy again, before I go?' he asked, trying to look angelic. 'I won't disturb her.'

'Just for a minute,' agreed Mrs Greer, 'while I chat to your mum.' Turning, she began to make arrangements to look after Mick while his mum was working late at the supermarket.

'I just could not refuse when they offered me the overtime,' Mick's mum said. 'What with things the way they have been since his dad went. I'll pay you a bit extra, mind you. I'm not asking you to do favours for nothing.'

Mrs Greer and Mrs Browning, Mick's mum, settled the details. Mick did not mind at all. He would be able to have more time with Sandy. Even more time with John would not be too bad. In fact, he half wished he could stay at the Greers' all the time. Home wasn't the same without Dad. He had hated moving to the flat when their old house had been sold. Why did he have to live there, and not in a nice house like John's? It was horrible walking home from John's, leaving behind the neat streets and gardens and watching the blocks of flats loom up in front of him.

There was always a load of rubbish blowing around in a never-ending circle just by the entrance to the flats. The stairway smelt awful, like a mixture of smelly socks and rotten cabbage leaves, no matter how many times Mum scrubbed the steps with disinfectant. As if that was not bad enough, Mum was always tired, his two older sisters were a pain, Dad was not bothered with him any more. In fact he would be better off here living with John.

Mum's voice broke through his thoughts.

'Time to go, Mick.'

'I don't want to,' he mumbled, 'I'm staying here.' He

wished Mum would take off her shop overall before she came to collect him.

'Now don't give me any of that talk. I've had a long day. Find your anorak and move.' Mum pushed him hard in the middle of the back. He nearly fell over.

I do not care, he thought. They can all get at me. It does not matter any more. I'm going to have my own puppy. Sandy is going to be mine, all mine.

He thought of her lovely little face, staring at him earlier that afternoon. No-one else knew it yet, but that meeting would change his life.

'Sorry, Mum,' Mick smiled at her. 'I'll catch you up. My anorak's down the garden.'

He ran to fetch it and stopped on the way back to bend down by Sandy's bed.

'Night-night, little Sandy. I love you,' he said so quietly no-one else could hear. Sandy's tail twitched in reply before she shut her eyes and went off to sleep.

'Mum,' said Mick the next morning. 'Do you like dogs?'

'Well, they're okay, in the right place and with the right people,' replied Mum, wrapping her fingers around her hot mug of coffee.

'What do you mean?' asked Mick.

'Dogs are fine for people with lots of time to look after them properly and with enough space to let them run around; not to mention enough money to feed them and pay vets' bills.'

'Is Mrs Greer's house a right place?' Mick asked again.

'Mrs Greer's is ideal,' said Mum. A thought suddenly struck her. 'You don't mind going there, do you? I thought you liked it.'

'Course I like it,' smiled Mick. Now it was time for the big question. 'Mum, can I have a puppy?' he said quickly.

Mum had not heard. She had started to clear the

breakfast things.

'What did you say?'

'I said,' Mick stood up and went over to her, 'I said, can I have a puppy?'

'You must be daft,' replied Mum. 'You know what things are like here. There's no way you can have a pup.'

'But I want one so much.' Mick kicked his trainers against the chair leg. 'You don't understand!'

'Look, Mick, whether I understand or not makes no difference. I don't want a pup. We can't afford a pup. It's not fair to have one in a flat. There's no-one to look after it during the day. You are not having one – do I make myself clear?'

'But Mum . . . just a little one . . . like Sandy,' begged Mick.

'Oh, that's what's brought this on, has it?' Mum was getting cross. 'Every time John has something, you want it. Last week it was model ships, this week it's dogs!'

'It's not like that, Mum. It's different.' Mick did not know how best to argue with her. When you are nine years old, grown-ups always get their own way.

'Look. I don't want to hear any more about it. Go and bang on Claire and Emma's door. They'll be late again!'

At that moment Claire came into the room. She was sixteen and went to college to learn to be a secretary. Mick thought she looked like a walking rag-bag. The latest trend at college was to paint your own designs onto plain clothes. Claire was wearing an enormous baggy T-shirt with a zebra painted on it. Mick could tell it was a zebra by the stripes. Without those it looked more like a cross-eyed camel caught in a snow-storm. The outfit was completed by bright yellow trousers, a pair of flip-flops and a black shawl Claire had bought at a jumble sale for ten pence. To set it all off, she had tied a clump of hair on top of her head, with what looked like a football boot lace.

'Off to the zoo?' Mick inquired.

'Shut up,' snapped Claire, grabbing a piece of dry toast. 'Got to go. Mustn't be late for typing. See you.'

'Hey, Claire, that's my boot lace.' Mick jumped up. 'We've got football today. Mr Hinds will kill me if I haven't got my boots.' He took a flying leap at his sister. She just dodged and banged out of the front door.

'Mum, what about my laces?' Mick complained to Mum.

'You'll have to make do.' Mum was in a rush now. 'I've got to go. Make sure you lock the door when you go out . . . and wash these dishes up.' She dropped a well-aimed kiss on his head, slipped her coat on, yelled to Emma once more to get up and went off to work.

Mick just sat there. Mornings got worse. When Dad had been here, it was a lot better.

Just then Emma emerged from her room ready for work. She was really old – twenty. Soon she would have saved up enough money to get married to David. Mick thought Emma was a drip but David was okay. He had taken Mick round the block on his motor-bike last week and let him help to change a wheel. Why he would want to marry Emma was a mystery. She hated motor-bikes, noise, dirt — and young brothers!

'Where's the cornflakes?' she asked, sitting down gracefully at the table.

'Gone,' answered Mick.

'Gone! There were loads left yesterday.'

'Well, I had three bowlsful today,' Mick replied.

'You greedy little toad! For a skinny wimp, I don't know where you put all this food.'

'I'm not a wimp! My arm muscles have grown one centimetre since Easter. Look. I measured them.' He rolled up his sleeve to reveal a bony forearm.

'Very impressive, I'm sure.' Emma poured herself a glass of milk.

'Em, you like dogs, don't you?' Mick thought it might be good to get someone on his side.

'Yes, they're cute. Why?'

'I want one,' replied Mick.

'You'll be lucky! You'll have to wait until you've grown-up and left home. When David and I get married, we're going to have a cat – cream and brown I think to match the colours in the living room – mind you, I'm not sure yet about the brown . . .'

Emma was off again!

Mick did the washing up after Emma left to catch the bus to town. As he made the bubbles froth over the side of the bowl by beating them furiously with a fork, he began to think. Mum had said 'no' to a dog. He was cross. If they did not have to live in this awful dump, he was sure he could have had a dog. It was not fair. Why should John live in his big posh house and have a garden all for himself, when the four of them had to squash into this place? It was Dad's fault for leaving them and making them sell their old home.

Anyway, Mum might change her mind. He could be extra nice to her for a few days, starting now. After finishing the drying-up, he tidied the kitchen, not noticing the time until the kitchen clock pinged. A quarter to nine! 'Late again,' he gasped, and dashed out of the flat arriving at school with ten seconds to spare.

How am I ever going to get Sandy, he thought, as they got into straggly lines in the playground. Mr Hinds was on duty and, as he repeatedly rang the bell for silence, Mick remembered he had forgotten his boots for football. More trouble ahead! At least at four o'clock he would able to see Sandy and perhaps play with her. Tonight he could find time to make a plan. Get Sandy! he could call it. It would be like a secret operation in the war. Yes that's what I'll call it. 'Operation Sandy!'

2

The bell marking the end of school for the day had not finished ringing before Mick was out of the classroom door.

'Come on, John,' he shouted. 'Your mum might have brought Sandy to meet us.'

'You don't know nothing,' replied John. 'She can't come out yet. She has to have some injections first.'

'Injections! Is she ill or something?' Mick paused in his headlong rush. Surely Sandy could not be ill already?

'I told you – you don't know nothing,' John stated importantly. 'She has to have some injections to stop her getting a terrible dog disease. When she has had some of them she can go anywhere.'

Mick slowed down and waited for his friend.

'What else did your mum tell you?' he asked. There was obviously more to having a pup than he had realized.

'Well, she is a very important puppy. One day she will belong to a blind person and help them to get to places. While she is a pup she lives with a special family, ours, and we start to train her.' John trotted out the information he had been told.

'How can you train her?' Mick was puzzled.

John turned to him. 'We teach her to be a good dog, do what she is told and get used to lots of different people and places. It's called puppy walking. Come on. Race you to the corner.'

As usual Mick won. John was a lot slower than him, and ran along behind Mick like a steam engine. Mrs Greer was waiting for them. She always looked smart, like someone out of a television programme.

'How's Sandy?' Mick blurted out.

'Fine. She's waiting at home for her next meal. You can give it her if you like.' Mrs Greer smiled at them. 'How's today been?'

'Mick got told off by Hinds again,' said John. Mick tried to kick him to shut him up but missed. John carried on talking away – mostly about how good he had been at school and what a day-dream Mick was.

'Let's play "Treasure" again tonight, shall we?' asked John, as they reached his home.

'I don't know. I've got to do some lines for Mr Hinds,' lied Mick. The only way to be on his own was to pretend he had work to do. 'I'll play after. Can I feed Sandy now, Mrs Greer?'

'Of course. She'll have two Weetabix and some warm milk. Don't make it too hot for her.'

'Weetabix?' said Mick puzzled.

'Yes. Twice a day she has milky cereal and twice a day she has a soft meat meal.'

Sandy was scampering round the kitchen. Mick could not stop looking at her. Her paws were enormous and seemed to flop up and down every time she walked. Her little tail, like a piece of worn rope, wagged from side to side.

'Wake up, day-dream,' said Mrs Greer.

Mick quickly made the mushy cereal and watched in delight as Sandy half ate and half drank it. The food went all over her nose and some stuck on her floppy ears.

'Let Mick do his lines now,' said Mrs Greer to John. 'You go and watch telly for a bit.'

Mick sat at the dining room table and got out an old exercise book. At the top of a clean page he wrote 'THE PROBLUM' in capital letters. Then he wrote 'OPERATION SANDY'. He stared out of the window waiting for an idea to come. It was a nice window to look through. The garden looked lovely. Not like the horrible view from the flat. There all he could see were even more flats. He sighed and brought his mind back to the problem. Drawing a line with his ruler he wrote:

1. Sandy sort of belongs to John's family.
2. Sandy really belongs to the Guide Dog people.
3. Mum says I can't have a dog.
4. I've got £4.37 pence.

Mick chewed his pencil for a while then he wrote 'Top Secret' right across the page. Writing the list had not helped a lot. He still did not know what to do.

Suddenly he remembered that Steve, his teacher at church, had told him that he should talk to God about his problems. He screwed his face up, eyes tight shut and prayed 'Please God, give me an idea. Amen,' and sat back and waited. Nothing happened. Never mind. He would give God until Sunday to come up with an idea.

Mrs Greer called him for tea. John's dad was home now. It made it worse really. Mick missed his own dad so much that sometimes it hurt, like a tummy-ache but higher up.

I wish he had not gone, thought Mick for the thousandth time. He tried not to think about those awful scenes before Dad left. Mum crying, Dad shouting, doors slamming. Now Dad lived miles away with a new wife. Mick only saw him in the holidays and sometimes at week-ends.

'You all right, Mick?' Mr Greer's voice broke into his thoughts.

'Yes, thank you,' he replied. 'I don't think I'm hungry.' He pushed the pasta and rich meat sauce round his plate.

'It's all right, Mick,' said Mrs Greer kindly. 'How about some chocolate ice cream?'

Mick's face brightened visibly. 'Great,' he replied and the hurt inside began to fade as he and John raced to eat the most ice-cream.

'Can we play with Sandy now?' he asked.

'Okay.'

Released into the garden, they went mad! Sandy charged round the lawn, sniffing at the grass. Now and then she would jump in the air, like a young lamb. She tried to bite the heads off some flowers but they were too tough for her.

Then she saw a bee and decided to investigate. As she kept following it from flower to flower, the boys trailed behind her. She tried to catch it with her paw but missed every time.

'Let's teach her to play ball,' suggested John.

'Good idea,' agreed Mick.

Sandy soon learned to chase the ball but not to bring it back. They had great fun diving for the pup and rolling over in the grass with her. Then Mick grabbed the ball and threw it hard. 'Fetch! Sandy. Fetch!' he yelled. The ball flew down the garden and over the hedge at the bottom.

'You idiot,' said John. 'It's gone in Mr Thomas's again. He'll kill us. You'll have to crawl through the hedge and fetch it.'

'I can't,' replied Mick, 'the gap's too little.'

'I'll give you a shove.' John pushed hard. Mick managed to get into Mr Thomas's garden and started to search for the ball. At that moment Sandy decided this was a good new game. She easily got through the hedge and discovered the wonderful world of Mr Thomas's vegetable patch.

'Oh, heck,' gasped Mick, 'what shall we do now?'

'Catch her, you wally,' shouted John.

'I'm trying. She's too fast. You come and help.'

'I'm too big. Look, get her off his carrots.'

Sandy was chewing the tender tops off the carrots. Mick dived at her, missed and landed in an awful, prickly, gooseberry bush. He picked himself up, saw the ball and threw it back over the hedge, and carried on chasing Sandy.

All the noise brought old Mr Thomas out.

'I've told you boys before to keep out my garden.' He was really angry. 'What's that dog doing at my seedlings?'

The dog in question was rolling on them. Mr Thomas scooped her up in his big crinkly hands and dropped her back over the hedge. Then he grabbed Mick and heaved him back into John's garden.

'If you or that dog come into my garden again, I'll make you wish you had not been born,' he hissed.

Mr Greer heard the angry voice and came down the garden. He managed to calm Mr Thomas down and promised to put some wire netting along the hedge, to keep Sandy in. He told Mr Thomas that the boys would each give him two pounds for the ruined seedlings. John protested that it was not his fault but a look from his father soon shut him up.

'We cannot leave you alone for five minutes before you're in trouble,' Mr Greer grumbled. 'Now go in and take Sandy with you.'

Sandy was filthy. Her pale golden coat was covered in mud and seedlings. Mick and John were allowed to bath her. She hated it and wriggled while they held her in the old baby bath. Then Mick wrapped her in a big soft towel and rubbed her dry.

He felt so happy. He loved Sandy more than ever. She was falling asleep on his lap. Tenderly he stroked her golden head. He was no nearer having her for his own. But one day she would be his – she must be.

On Sunday morning Mick got out his exercise book and found the page headed 'THE PROBLUM'. He read through it. Only one thing had changed since Thursday. Glumly he crossed out 'I've got £4.37 pence' and wrote – 'only £2.37 pence now' in its place. Mum had insisted that he paid Mr Thomas out of his own money. She had been cross, when she had fetched him later on Thursday evening. He had scratched himself and had ripped the front of his jumper crawling through the hedge.

Being nice to Mum was not working too well. Still, today might be better – it could not be worse.

I'll make her breakfast in bed, he thought.

Mick decided to boil an egg for Mum and make bread and butter fingers. He would do one for himself and make a big pot of tea. The fingers were soon done and he popped the eggs into the boiling water.

I'll just run downstairs, he thought, and find her some flowers. By the flats there was some open ground with a few benches on it, a broken roundabout and a good climbing frame. Here Mick picked some buttercups and red clover before running back upstairs. He stuffed the flowers into a mug, put them on a tray and decided that the eggs were done.

When it was ready, he went to Mum's room. Surely she would like this. As he opened the door he felt the, by now familiar, ache. He still expected Dad to be there as well, but no. Mum was alone. She looked younger, happier somehow. Her dark hair was tousled and all over the pillow. She kept it tied back in the day time. Normally she looked old and worried, always dashing off somewhere, in the same old coat. It was nice to see her smiling.

'Hello, love,' said Mum.

'I've done your breakfast,' said Mick, not looking at her.

'Oh, that's lovely.' Mum seemed genuinely pleased.

'Why don't you pop into bed next to me and have yours.'

Mick jumped in. When Dad was here, he had often got into their bed in the morning. Since he had left, Mick had not wanted to. Now he realized how much he loved his mum.

'Love you,' he muttered, through a spoonful of rather runny egg.

'I love you, as well,' said Mum. 'I'm sorry I've been so busy and tired lately. I'm still getting used to this job. Oh, Mick, it's been hard for all of us this last year. I still miss your dad, you know.'

'So do I,' mumbled Mick.

'Well, he's not coming back, so we had better make the best of it – eh?'

'Yes, Mum,' replied Mick. It was the first time Mum had told him how she felt. She was treating him almost like a grown-up. It made him feel quite important.

'Are we going to church today?'

'I'd like to. It seems much more important to me nowadays to go and learn more about God and be with other people who know him,' said Mum. One of the changes since Dad went had been going to church. He had overheard Mum telling Mrs Greer that she had rediscovered her faith, whatever that meant.

'Yes,' he replied, after a pause. 'Steve, who takes our class, is good fun. I like finding out about Jesus. Steve told us he is always with us and answers our prayers.' That reminded Mick he had given God until Sunday to come up with a plan for 'Get Sandy'. Today was his last chance.

They managed to get to church just in time. Mick ran off to sit with his mates after assuring Mum he would not whisper, fidget or eat sweets during the talk.

Today was a Family Service. Everybody stayed together for the hour, instead of the children going off to their classes.

Mick sat on his hard seat and wriggled around. They were singing some songs with lots of actions for the little children. He was not going to pretend to be an elephant or kangaroo today! Then some of the older teenagers did a piece of music. It was very loud. The drummer nearly gave himself a fit banging away. The girl singer looked like someone off 'Top of the Pops' and kept saying 'He brings peace' over and over again.

Soon it was time for the talk. Mick was getting restless. Where was the idea from God? Pretending to be animals or thinking about 'peace' was not much help.

The vicar switched on an overhead projector. Some writing was beamed on to the screen. Mick, along with everyone else, was asked to read it out aloud.

'You do not have what you want because you do not ask God for it. And when you ask, you do not receive it, because your motives are bad; you ask for things to use for your own pleasures.'

Then the speaker went on to tell them that it was two verses from the Bible. He began to tell stories of how God had answered prayers. In the Bible people had prayed and God had done amazing things. Sick people got better, people were released from prison, or saved from shipwrecks. The vicar went on to tell them of how God answered prayers today. They had prayed for good weather for the Sunday School outing and the sun had shone all day. Lonely old Mrs Jones had asked God to give her new friends, when she had moved, and now she knew lots of people. The Hugheses' dog had been run over and everyone thought he would die. They had prayed in Sunday School and Spot was getting better.

At the mention of Spot, Mick really sat up and took notice. Peter Hughes was the same age as him. He knew how worried Peter had been after the accident and now Spot was hobbling around. If God could answer a prayer for Peter and Spot, he could answer one for Mick and

Sandy.

The vicar said he had some important things to say about the second part of the verse. By then Mick had switched off. God had answered his prayer for an idea. He didn't need to have an idea! All he needed to do was to ask God to give him Sandy. That was all. 'Please God, give me Sandy,' he prayed over and over again.

Mick felt happy. It would all work out now.

The talk came to an end.

'Let's all read these verses out loud again,' said the vicar. 'They are found in the book of James, chapter four and verses two and three.'

Mick had brought his Good News Bible with him. Steve had given it to him when he had started to come to church. Where on earth was James? There it was. Right near the back. He marked the page with a sweet paper.

As soon as they got back home, Mick ran into his room and slammed the door shut.

'Hey, what you doing?' shouted Claire, who was cooking dinner. 'Come on, out of there at once and help me.'

'Leave him alone,' said Mum. 'He's excited about something. Now don't you go and spoil it. He wants to do something in his room.'

'Not clean it, I suppose,' grinned Claire.

Mick was busy. He got a clean piece of paper, rested it on a 'Whizzo' annual and sat on the bed. Carefully he wrote 'Sandy' in each corner. Then he tried to draw a dog on the paper. It was a bit wobbly but he knew it was a dog. Turning to his Bible, he opened it at the sweet-paper marker. Brown gobs of toffee were sticking the pages together. He licked his finger and rubbed until the worst of the mess was gone. At least he would have no difficulty finding James chapter four again!

In his very best writing, which even Mr Hinds would

have liked, he copied out 'You do not have what you want because you do not ask God for it.' Then he thought. Finding a different coloured felt-tip pen that actually worked, he wrote 'Dear God, please can I have Sandy?' To finish it off, he added the date – Sunday 14th May.

Now he had said the prayer, lots of times, and he had written it down. God would be sure to take notice of it.

'Dinner in five minutes, Mick.' Mum's voice reached him.

He got up and stuck his prayer on the wall where he could easily read it. If he reminded God of it every day, it would work.

So every day Mick prayed his prayer, about twenty times, and every day after school he played with Sandy.

By now Sandy was getting used to wearing a collar. How she hated it at first! She would rub her neck along the floor trying to get the collar off. When that failed, she would try to grab the end of it, with her mouth, to chew it.

'It's cruel,' said Mick to Mrs Greer one evening. 'Why don't you leave it off her until she's older?'

'She's got to learn,' replied John's mum.

As usual she was right. One day Mick noticed that Sandy was wearing her collar with no fuss.

'Good girl,' he said, getting down on his knees and giving her a playful tickle.

As she rolled over, he noticed a new medallion on the collar: 'The Guide Dog for the Blind Association' and a picture of a dog's head. He turned it over and read the back: 'G.D.B.A. Puppy Walking Scheme'.

Mick's brain whirled. He read the words again. Sandy belonged to Guide Dogs. It said so. In metal. Engraved. How was God going to get Sandy for him now? He had half forgotten about the Guide Dog people.

'What's up?' asked Mrs Greer kindly. She had noticed

Mick being unnaturally quiet.

'Oh, nothing,' he said quickly. He would have to watch it. People would guess what he was planning if he was not more careful. He had better make sure he prayed his prayer, even more often.

Over the weeks Sandy learned to walk on the lead, to be obedient and not to bark every time she got excited. Mick was happy. If only God would hurry up and answer the prayer, things would be perfect. He had had a bit of a set-back with that. Mum had sat down on his bed one night with her serious look on her face.

'Mick, this prayer, for Sandy. It's impossible,' she had begun.

'Not to God,' interrupted Mick. 'He does impossible things.'

'Well, yes,' Mum paused, 'but not that impossible. Even if God gave you Sandy, you could not keep her. Let's get that straight. She will never be yours. Do you understand?'

Mick grunted by way of reply. He would not give up hope. God was greater than Mum! Taking his prayer off the wall, he hid it in his drawer. God would answer his prayer, it was just taking a bit of time. Perhaps by the end of the holidays?

3

'Has it come? Has it come?' shouted Mick, jumping up from the breakfast table.

'Hang on a minute,' said Emma, sleepily. 'Let me see . . . There's a bill here, Mum won't like that. One for me. Must be Dave again . . .'

'Get on with it,' interrupted Mick. 'Is mine there?' Emma skimmed a letter across the room and it landed, neatly, in Mick's bowl of cornflakes.

'You idiot!' he said half-heartedly, eager to read the letter. He let the milk drip off and wiped a few soggy cornflakes from it, with his hanky. Carefully he opened this week's letter from Dad. It was there. The coach tickets to take him to Dad's next Saturday. Two whole weeks with Dad. Mick could not wait. He began to read.

'Dear Mick, here are your coach tickets. Get Mum or one of the girls to put you on the coach. Tell the driver that Pamela will meet you. Don't talk to strangers. You'd better take a snack with you, as it's a long journey. I'll see you after work, love from Dad.' Mick read it through again. Why did Pamela have to meet him, not Dad? He could not stand her. No way was he going to call her 'Aunty Pamela'. She was not his aunty. She was Dad's new wife.

Still he was not going to let 'her', as he always called Pamela, spoil his holiday with Dad. Two whole weeks, just Dad and him.

The next week dragged by. The school holidays had started and Mick spent the time at John's house. Most days were the same. They played a bit, went swimming, ate a lot and took Sandy for long walks. On the Friday evening, Mick managed to escape from John. Taking Sandy with him, he crawled into his favourite bush.

'I've got to go away,' he told her solemnly. 'You be a good girl until I get back. I love you. You'll soon be mine now.' He held her very close. A small tear trickled down his cheek as he kissed her goodbye. Sandy licked it up with her rough pink tongue. Just then Mrs Greer called to tell him it was time to go. 'Bye, again,' he whispered to Sandy.

Mick had never been on the coach trip alone and was excited about it. Mum took him to the coach station. She kept on and on. 'Mind your manners . . . eat what you're given . . . be good on the coach . . . phone me up when you get there . . .'

At last it was time to get on the coach. Mum told the poor driver about a hundred times that he must look after Mick. He was travelling alone and would be met at the other end. The driver finally convinced her Mick would be all right. He sat him on a front seat and promised to keep an eye on him. This satisfied Mum, who gave him yet another sloppy kiss and, much better, a bag of sweets.

They were off! Mick waved wildly to Mum and then turned his attention to the journey. Every few minutes he patted his anorak pocket. It was there. His, by now very screwed up, prayer for Sandy.

The time passed quickly and Mick started to feel a bit panicky inside. What if he could not find Pamela? Or if the coach was late, and she had gone? When he did find her, what would he say to her? Oh, why could not Dad have met him?

His legs felt wobbly as he got up, ready to get off the bus. He need not have worried. There was Pamela. In bright red dungarees, waving madly. He could hardly miss her. She did not look much older than Emma.

As he jumped off the step, she caught him in a great big hug. Mick stiffened. He noticed she smelled really good.

'Hello, Mick. Great to see you. Let's find your luggage,' said Pamela. He stood still, not knowing what to say, as the driver unearthed his haversack. Pamela seemed not to notice. She rattled on about what they were going to do together. He only answered when she asked him what his favourite foods were. At least he would make sure sausage, egg and chips turned up regularly.

The drive from the station was quite short and soon Mick found himself in a clean, tidy bedroom, staring out of the window. He had not noticed before but Dad's new house had a long, thin garden behind it. Long, thin gardens are ideal for dogs. A new idea sprang into Mick's mind. He could ask Dad if he could keep a dog, his Sandy, here. That would solve things.

Hearing a car pull into the driveway, Mick ran to the bedroom door and then, suddenly, he stopped. He so much wanted to see Dad, yet now he felt nervous. Dad might not really want him here. I want to go home, he thought, missing Mum all of a sudden. He did not have time to think any more. Heavy footsteps bounded up the stairs, two at a time. The door was flung open and there stood Dad. His arms were wide apart and, automatically, Mick ran into them. Mick could feel the strong arms squeezing him as if they would never let him go. Dad's jacket was hairy and tickled his face, which was squashed into it.

'Oh, Dad, Dad,' was all he could say, while Dad just carried on hugging him.

'Right then, you two, how about some tea?' Pamela came into the room and put her arms across them both. Mick sprang back. It was not right. She should not be here, with her arm round them. It should have been

Mum. Her words came back to him '. . . he's not coming back. We had better make the best of it.' They prayed together, every night, that they would make the best of it. Now it was up to Mick to act in the best way. Silently he prayed, 'Help me, Jesus, to put up with Pamela.'

'I'm starving,' he said aloud.

Over tea Dad told him that he had got a few days off work, so they would be able to do lots of things together.

'Let's make a list of what to do,' suggested Dad. They spent until bedtime deciding where to go, having a friendly argument about which was the best football team in England. Mick did not mind what they did. All that mattered was that he was with Dad.

At bedtime Mick realized how tired he was and quickly got undressed in the strange bedroom. When he was ready, Dad came up to say good-night.

'Happy?' he asked.

'Yes, Dad,' replied a sleepy Mick.

'I love you very much, Mick. Do you know that?'

Strange question, thought Mick. 'Um,' he mumbled.

'I just want you to know that. Although it didn't work out for me and your Mum to stay together, it doesn't mean that I don't love you any more. It's great to have you here. See you in the morning.' Dad bent over the bed and ruffled his hair before leaving the room, just as he used to do, before he left home.

Mick was not quite sure what he was on about. Only one thing mattered. Dad loved him. Well, two things mattered, he thought. He still had to 'Get Sandy'. He would talk to Dad about it. Dad would solve it. 'Thanks, God, for giving me another idea,' he said, before rolling onto his side and falling off to sleep.

4

The next few days were marvellous. Better than anything Mick had imagined. Dad was there all the time. Whatever Mick wanted to do, he could. They visited a transport museum, the zoo, watched a real cricket match, played endless games of football in the park and all went swimming at the local leisure centre.

Mick began to think that living here would be better than at home, with Mum and the girls. If he lived here, Dad would do great things with him all the time. Even Pamela was not that bad. She let him stay up late to watch cowboy films on the telly. The food she cooked was ace. Chips nearly every day! Of course, she was not like his own mum but, as grown-ups went, she could be fun. Mind you, he did not fancy having to go to a different school and leaving all his mates behind. It was best not to think about that.

On the day before Dad went back to work, he and Mick set off early on a fishing trip. Mick had not been on a proper fishing trip before and he was excited about it. After walking from the car for what seemed miles, over the moor, Dad found the perfect spot. They set up base near the shade of a wrinkled old tree. Pamela had given them a huge basket of food, to keep them going. She was always saying how thin he looked.

Dad showed Mick how to bait his line with revolting, crawling maggots. Then they practised casting into the dark, quiet stream. Mick could not get the hang of it. First his maggots flew off, then he got his hook stuck in the stream bank, before getting his line tangled around a bush. Dad would think he was a right idiot.

'Right, let's try again,' said Dad patiently. 'Just take it easy. Don't go at it so mad.'

Finally, following Dad's instructions, Mick got his hook, float and maggots all in the water. All at roughly the right place. Dad expertly flicked his arm and his line joined Mick's.

The two sat there in friendly silence. This is perfect, thought Mick. The sunlight danced on the stream and the trees seemed to dip and bow into the cool water. High above them some bird was singing its head off. Otherwise it was so peaceful.

I want this to last forever, thought Mick. He leaned against Dad, kicked off his trainers and sat on the stream bank, dangling his feet in the water. I will ask him, he thought. He must say yes! He felt a bit scared. It was so important that Dad agreed to his request.

'Dad,' he began. 'Are you listening?'

'Mmm,' replied Dad. Well, at least he had not fallen asleep.

'Dad, can I come to live with you and have a dog?' The words tumbled out in a rush. There, he had said it.

Dad was surprised. He could not have heard right. 'What did you say?' he asked, giving Mick his full attention.

Mick looked up at Dad's face. 'I want to live with you,' he said, slowly and clearly. 'I want to have a dog too.'

There was a long silence that went on for ever. Mick tried to cross his toes and fingers, hoping, waiting, for the reply that would change his life.

'Can I, Dad?' he said at last.

Dad did not know how to answer his son. Mick would never understand the situation fully until he was older. However he tried to explain it, Mick would find it hard to accept.

'Mick,' he began, gently, holding the boy's arm. 'Mick, you know you can't live here with me and Pamela. Not all the time.'

'But, why, Dad, why?' Mick cried out. 'I want to. I do. Really.'

'You want to now because you've had such a nice holiday. It would not be like this normally. I work long hours, get tired. I could not take you out all the time . . .' Dad stumbled to a stop.

'I don't care,' Mick was getting desperate. 'I just want to be here.'

'What about Mum . . . and Emma . . . and Claire?' asked Dad. Mick was silent. He was not too bothered about Emma and Claire, but Mum . . . that was a different matter. He needed her. He needed Dad too. He felt like he was being torn in half. His happiness of a few minutes ago had disappeared.

'Anyway,' Dad continued. 'Your Mum has got custody of you three children. You could not live here anyway.'

'Custard?' said Mick, not hearing correctly. What was Dad talking about custard for?

'Custody,' Dad smiled as he corrected him. 'It's like a law. Mum has you during the week. I can see you at week-ends and school holidays. It's a law. We can't change it. Anyway you are better off with Mum.'

Mick was devastated. He tried as hard as he could not to cry. He would not let Dad think he was a baby. Sitting there he felt awful. None of his plans worked. God was not helping him at all. 'Get Sandy' was no nearer happening.

Dad looked at his sad face. He must change the subject. This conversation was becoming a disaster.

'What did you say about a dog?' he asked.

'Well, I can't have one in the flat. Can I have one

here? I would look after it, by myself, in the holidays.' Mick did not think there was much hope of getting what he wanted.

'I don't see why not,' said Dad, glad that he could do something to please Mick. 'Nice to have a dog about the place.'

Mick could hardly believe his ears.

'Really?' he said. 'Honest?' He jumped up and hugged Dad wildly. The fishing rods were knocked over, but neither of them noticed. 'You mean it? Do you mean it?'

'Well, it should be all right,' said Dad. 'I'll tell you what, we'll go down the Dogs' Home and see what they've got. Let's pack this lot up. The fish aren't biting today.'

'No,' said Mick. Going down to the Dogs' Home would never do. 'I don't want to. I want to choose one, myself, at my home. Please, let me get it myself.' He did not want any old dog. It had got to be Sandy.

'Okay,' agreed Dad. He was just pleased that the miserable boy of a few minutes ago was happy.

Mick charged round with happiness, jumping in the air, leaping over the fishing rods and making a tremendous din. His activities were brought to a sudden halt when he slipped, and fell into the stream. That was when he discovered that the water was rather muddy.

Dad hauled him out, helped him out of all his wet clothes and dressed him in his own jumper. He did look funny, walking back to the car. Dad's jumper came down to his knees and was miles too wide. He felt like a scarecrow but that did not stop his happiness bubbling up inside him. He could have a dog! Now all he had to do was to 'Get Sandy' and keep her here.

Pamela met them at the door. She took one look at Mick, sniffed and ordered him off to the bath.

'Dad says I can have a dog,' Mick told her excitedly.

'I can keep her here. He says so.'

Pamela went still. She did not seem to share his excitement.

'Oh, he does, does he?' she said in a curious flat voice. 'Now get on up to that bath.' She waited a minute as Mick went upstairs. Then Mick heard her say to Dad, 'I think we had better have a talk.'

What were they going to talk about? Mick was desperate with curiosity. Pamela seemed quite upset. He crept downstairs to listen. They seemed to have forgotten he was supposed to be in the bath. He curled up on the stairs into a tight ball. Hidden by the banisters, they could not see him.

The door to the living room was nearly shut. Mick could not hear everything that was being said.

'I could not say no. Not when he looked so upset . . .' That was Dad. Pamela was speaking too softly for Mick to overhear. Dad's voice boomed out again. 'Well. How was I to know that you'd feel like that! I was only trying to do my best.'

Pamela was getting worked up. As her voice got higher and higher, Mick, in his hiding place, heard more of what she was saying.

'I can't stand dogs! I've got enough to do without having a stupid, smelly animal around the place. Have you forgotten about the baby? I can't cope with being pregnant and having a scruffy mongrel.'

Mick half wished he was not listening. What was this about the baby? Surely Pamela was not having one. She was not fat enough. And, anyway, Sandy was not a scruffy mongrel. She was beautiful.

'You will have to tell him,' shouted Pamela. 'Tell him you made a mistake. I don't care if it was a promise.'

As he heard her, Mick burst from his hiding place and stormed into the room.

'I heard. I heard,' he yelled. 'You don't need to tell

me. I hate you. I hate you.' He dashed out of the room, tears pouring down his dirty cheeks. Mick rushed upstairs to the bathroom and locked the door. No one could get him here. As he ran the steaming water, Dad came and banged on the door.

'Let me explain,' he pleaded. 'Open the door, Mick, I can explain.'

Mick refused to answer. No explanation would be good enough. He got in the bath and heard Pamela come upstairs. Not her as well! He hated the sight of her. Curly hair, flowery dress and long pink finger-nails. It was her fault.

'We'll leave you to calm down,' she said, through the closed door. Then there was silence.

Mick lay like a statue in his bath. His world had fallen apart. Only an hour ago he could have a dog. Now he could not. He was worn out with all of today's emotions. It was not fair. No-one was bothered with him. No-one cared about him. With clenched fists he rubbed his tired, streaming eyes. He had never imagined he could feel as sad as this. All his hopes were dashed. He was alone. No-one to share his terrible heartache.

As he sat there in the rapidly cooling water, he remembered something Steve had said one Sunday at church. About Jesus always being with you. He cared. 'Oh, Jesus,' he sobbed, 'I'm so lonely. Please be with me. Please let me know you care.' For once he didn't ask for Sandy. He was too sad even to mention her name.

5

Dad and Pamela did lots of explaining. They told Mick all about the new baby that would be born around Christmas-time. He was not interested. Babies were boring. Dogs were a lot more fun. Dad told him, carefully and patiently, why he could not keep a dog there. He kept telling him that he was sorry. Mick listened but found it very hard to forgive Dad. Pamela and Dad were being extra nice to him but Mick knew they were only trying to make it up to him. When the end of his time at Dad's finally came, Mick was not sorry to leave. He had had enough of Pamela going on about the new baby.

Dad took him to the coach station. At least he did not fuss about like Mum. They got there too early, so Dad took him for a drink of pop. As they sat in the station cafe, Dad said, 'The new baby, Mick makes no difference. I'll still love you as much as ever, you know.'

Mick sat quietly kicking the table legs and trying to blow bubbles into his pop down the bendy straw. If Dad really loved him, why had he left home? It did not make sense. However making the best of it meant believing what Dad said. He stared at Dad. Funny, he had never noticed all the crinkles in his face before, and his hair was starting to go grey.

'I love you too,' he eventually replied. 'When are you coming to see me again?' Dad wrote down some dates on a page ripped out of his diary and passed it to Mick.

'I'm really sorry about the dog,' he began.

Mick interrupted. 'It's okay, Dad. I understand it would never have worked out.'

'You'll have to have one when you've grown up,' said Dad, standing up. 'Come on, time to go.'

The journey home was long and boring . At last there was Mum waiting to meet him. It was great to see her again. He did not mind the sloppy kiss this time. She asked him loads of questions about what he had done. He told her nearly everything. It was best not to tell her about the day on the moor with Dad. She would only be upset if she knew he had wanted to stay there forever.

In fact, Mick realized later, as he flopped into bed, he was glad to be home. Even Claire and Emma seemed pleased to see him. They wanted to know all about Pamela and the new baby. Mum seemed to know about it already.

Straight after breakfast, Mum took Mick to John's house. Mick had missed John but not as much as he had missed Sandy. How she had grown! She jumped into his outstretched arms and began to lick him all over. She had remembered him. Mick had been half afraid she would forget him, but he need not have worried.

Sandy's training was progressing well. Mrs Greer and the boys took her to lots of different places that summer. It was very important that she learned to get used to noise, crowds, various smells, cars and buses. Mick liked these trips. Often he held Sandy's lead. He could pretend she was his dog then.

Mrs Greer was good fun. She always had time to take the boys out and she always managed to look smart as well. Perhaps it was because she did not have to work all day, like Mick's mum.

All too soon the holidays were over. Life was back to normal. School, work, more school. The highlight of each day for Mick was seeing Sandy. Every evening he went with the Greers for a long walk with her. She did what he told her. He was sure she knew he was special. By now she was quite big and had lost her baby puppy look. John and Mick had taught her to play football. She would push the ball along with her head, steering it past objects and through whatever they were using as goal posts. It was great fun.

'I don't know what use it will be having a guide dog who can play football!' joked Mrs Greer.

Mick wished she would not keep on talking about Sandy as a guide dog. He wanted to forget that she belonged to them. He still prayed that he would 'Get Sandy' but nothing seemed to be happening. The weeks and months were zooming by and Sandy was getting more precious to him every day.

In no time at all, it was Christmas. Mick gave Sandy a gift-wrapped bone which she enjoyed a lot. He had some nice presents but the best thing of all was when Dad came to visit. He took him to a pantomime, which was brill. Then they went out for a proper meal, to a restaurant, afterwards.

'How are you, these days?' asked Dad. 'Forgiven me yet, about the dog?'

'Of course,' said Mick through a mouthful of trifle. 'Anyway John lets me play with his dog a lot.' He told Dad all about Sandy. Well, not quite all. Not the bit about believing he would 'Get Sandy' for his very own. Dad told him Pamela was very tired. Her baby would be born soon. Perhaps Mick would like to come and stay at half-term in February? Mick would, and so it was all arranged.

After Dad went back to his home, Mick felt the holidays drag on. All his friends had dads who were there all the time. Their dads took them out, mended broken Christmas presents and had lots of laughs with them. Claire was looking after Mick while Mum worked. Mick preferred it at John's but Mum said 'no.' Claire could, for once, make herself useful. As far as Mick went, that meant he amused himself all day, while Claire lazed around reading magazines or blasted out her pop records fit to burst your eardrums.

Mick was almost pleased to go back to school. At least there was John's to go to. He loved going back into their warm home and sitting by the fire. Sandy would lie across his legs, as he and John played board games or watched television.

'It's amazing,' said Mrs Greer one evening, looking up from her knitting.

'What is?' asked John.

'Well, she's nearly ten months old now. Not a little puppy any more,' replied Mrs Greer. 'I'm going to really miss her.'

Mick began to take notice of the conversation. Miss her! What did she mean?

'Has she got to go?' asked John. He loved Sandy too. Not as much as Mick did but he still loved her.

'Of course she has,' said his mum. 'You know all about that.'

'But I don't want her to go,' complained John.

Mick pretended to be reading a comic. In reality his mind was working overtime. *John* did not want her to go! What about *him*?

'None of us wants her to go,' said Mrs Greer, 'but it has to happen. She's ready for her next bit of training now. We cannot do that. She needs the proper guide dog teachers.'

'When's she going?' asked John.

'She will be collected on Tuesday. They will bring us a new pup at the same time. He is all black and called Ben.'

Tuesday! Mick could not believe his ears. Tuesday! Today was Thursday. That meant in, let's see, in four, no five days' time, Sandy would be gone. No! No! he silently shouted. You cannot take her away. She's mine!

'Get Sandy' had not worked. He had asked God for

her and God had let him down. God had not answered his prayer at all. And now Sandy, his Sandy, was going to be taken away, He would never see her again. Mick's mind was in turmoil. What on earth could he do?

He looked at the beautiful, golden dog stretched out at his feet. She was asleep. Her nose and paws occasionally twitched. She was dreaming. Perhaps she was chasing Mick down to the brook, as she had done so often in the summer. Mick's heart was bursting with love for her. He could not lose her! He must not!

There was only one thing to do. God had not helped him. Mum and Dad were no use. He would have to do something himself. He would 'Get Sandy' and run away with her. Then she would be his. He had got until Monday to sort it out.

'It's okay, Sandy,' he whispered down her ear. 'You will be mine. Just trust me.'

6

'I'm going to the library,' shouted Mick on Saturday morning. 'I'll be ages.' He slammed the door behind him. He must be on his own. He must think. It was freezing outside and he slipped on an icy puddle. No use going down to the brook to think, today. He would freeze to death. They would discover his body lying there. Then they would be sorry. Everyone was against him. Well it was up to him. He would take Sandy and run away with her.

'What are you doing here, Mick Browning?' the librarian greeted him. Well, hardly 'greeted'. She had a face like thunder and Mick was sure she had not forgiven him for knocking a whole stack of books over, a few weeks ago.

'Come to change your books?' she continued.

Mick realized he had no books with him.

'No,' he replied politely. 'I've got to look some things up. For school. Can you tell me where the maps are?'

The librarian pointed to the far end of the room. Mick hunted unsuccessfully in his pockets. 'Can I have a piece of paper and a pencil?' he asked as nicely as he could.

'All right, but you had better be quiet.'

Mick helped himself to a huge stack of books and maps. Choosing a table in the corner, away from the old men slowly working their way through all of the daily newspapers, he got to work. He made a wall of books to hide his piece of paper and sat there, thinking. He thought and thought. It was easy to know what he had to do. Get Sandy, run away and keep her, forever. The hard bit was how to do it.

He leaned back on his chair, against the warmth of a radiator, and rammed his hands into his jeans pockets. He was sure there were a couple of toffees in there somewhere. His fingers closed round a sweet and dragged out a bit of paper with it. It was his 'Get Sandy' prayer. Fat lot of good that had been. Slowly he tore it up into tiny pieces. God was not interested. He was on his own.

He sat thinking for ages. Where could he run away too? It was no use just running. He had got to go somewhere.

Caravan. Funny word to come into his mind. Caravan – mmm – what could it mean? He had not been to a caravan for years. But – just a minute – the Greers had a caravan, somewhere. John was always boasting about going off for the weekend in the summer. He could take Sandy to the caravan. No-one went there in the winter. In fact, he remembered the Greers fetching a load of stuff from it way back, in the autumn. Shutting it up for the winter, they said.

Mick jumped up and ran to the door of the library. He would go and get the caravan key. He was sure he knew where it was kept. First drawer on the left, in the Greers' kitchen, along with a load of odds and ends.

'Hey, what are you doing?' The librarian grabbed the back of his anorak. 'What about all these books to put back?'

'I won't be long,' said Mick. 'Just got to get something.' He wriggled free and ran all the way to John's house.

Only Mr Greer was in. He looked funny. Usually Mick saw him in his smart business suit after work. Now he was wearing a baggy pair of green corduroy jeans, a brown jumper that was much too small, and he had not had a shave.

'Hello lad,' he said. 'My word, you look like you are in a hurry.'

'I am,' stated Mick. 'Look, I left something here last night. I need it. Can I look for it?'

'Okay – now calm down. I'll give you a hand.'

'Oh, no,' Mick replied quickly. 'It's okay. I'll find it. It's in the kitchen, I think,'

'What is?' asked Mr Greer kindly. He was a bit puzzled.

What indeed. Mick's brain was getting tired. 'The ke. . .' he began and quickly changed it to 'my pen for school.'

'Well, I'll make us a drink, while you look,' said Mr Greer.

That would never do. Mick had to get him out of the kitchen, and quick.

'Perhaps it's in John room,' he said.

Mr Greer said he would look. He did not want Mick messing up the room.

Quick as a flash, Mick reached into the kitchen drawer and rummaged around. His hand folded over the big cold key. Great! The label, with the address on it, was still tied to it. He stuffed it into his pocket and slammed the drawer shut. Just in time. Mr Greer returned.

'Can't find it, lad,' he stated. 'No luck yourself?'

'No,' said Mick, his heart bumping wildly. 'Must have lost it. I'd better go.'

He quickly rushed out of the front door. That was a close shave. He walked slowly back to the library.

'I told you I'd be back,' he said to old Thunderface.

Sitting at his table, he had a good look at the label. Good grief, it was foreign. Perhaps it was upside down. No. It was a weird-sounding place.

'Pen-y-bont', Owen's Caravan Site, Green Lane, Bodelwyddan.

Well it must be right. Where on earth was

Bodelwyddan?

Half an hour later, and with the help of one of the old men who had finished his newspaper, Mick found it. A village, in Wales, near Rhyl. Well, he had heard of Rhyl, so he would be able to find it. The old man told Mick lots of stories about holidays he had had at Rhyl, and how they used to walk for miles along the sand. Mick was not very interested, but then he realized the old man might be useful.

'How did you get there?' he interrupted.

'Charabanc, lad, always charabanc.'

Mick looked at him. He must be a nutter. 'Charabanc?' he asked.

'Well, you would call it a coach,' the old man replied. 'It was always charabanc to us. Even now I like the charabanc . . .'

Mick was not listening. Part two solved. He would get to this Bod . . . place on the coach. He knew all about coach travel. In the summer Dad had taught him how to look up timetables.

He jumped up, stuffed the books back onto the shelves, said goodbye to the old man who was talking to no-one in particular, and set off for the coach station.

It was a long cold walk and Mick was starving. He bought a huge currant bun and ate it as he walked along. He had not got enough money for a drink and was dying of thirst. At least it was warmer in the coach station. Eventually he found the timetables. It took ages to see when a coach went to Rhyl. There were not many of them but on Monday there was one at ten-thirty in the morning. That was cutting it a bit fine. It would have to do though.

Mick got home late in the afternoon. After three mugs of tea, he began to thaw out. He was tired, but happy. All this walking must be good for the brain. The great escape was working out. He had to have money, though.

And food. It was funny really, he was excited and scared at the same time. Excited because Sandy would soon be his and scared because stealing a dog and going to live miles away at the Bod-place was enough to frighten anyone. Still he had got to do it.

On Sunday morning, Mick pretended he had tummy-ache to get out of going to church. That got Mum out of the way. Emma was off out with David. Claire had been to a party last night and had come home very late. She had better stay in bed until at least dinner time.

Time to put the next part of his plan into action. Mick packed his haversack. One jumper, jeans and a change of underwear was enough. He needed to have plenty of room for more important things. He slid his torch down the side of the bag. Going to the kitchen cupboards, he decided what to take. Tins were really heavy. Better to leave them. He took some biscuits, a slab of cheese, a couple of packets of soup-mix and just one tin of baked beans. He would have to buy the rest of the food at the Bod-place.

Mick made himself eight ham and pickle sandwiches and wrapped them in a bread packet. They joined the rest of the stuff in his haversack. Grief, it was heavy already. And he needed dog-food. He hid the haversack under the bed.

So far so good. Now the tricky bit.

Kicking his slippers off, he tiptoed to his sisters' room. Quietly he opened the door. Claire was fast asleep, completely buried by her duvet. Ah, there it was. On the dressing table. Mum was always telling Emma not to leave money lying around. She got paid on Saturday, when the shop was closed, and could not put her money in the bank until Monday.

Mick reached out for the wage-packet, stubbing his big toe on Claire's discarded boots. 'Ee-er,' he groaned in agony.

Claire grunted and turned over in bed. Mick held his breath. Claire snorted again and went back to sleep.

Mick grabbed the money. He peeled off four of the five pound notes and put the rest back in the packet. He replaced it exactly as he had found it. Like a mouse he crept out of the room and into Mum's bedroom. Now where did she keep the electricity money? He knew she saved some money every week. One thing, no-one would rob her. He could not find it. In desperation he rifled through drawers, her wardrobe, under the bed and in the bed. Finally, in anger, he tipped her laundry basket out onto the floor. There it was. In a margarine tub marked electricity. He tipped the handful of money onto the bed. Good. Quite a few pound coins in with a load of change. Stuffing the money in his pocket, he looked round. Help! What a mess. She would be back soon. Mick had never moved so fast in his life. The room was nearly done when Mum came home. The bed was still a mess, so Mick lay on it.

'Hello,' shouted Mum. 'Feel better, Mick'

'Yes,' he replied in a pathetic weak voice. 'I'm in here.'

Mum entered her room. 'My word,' she said, 'you must have been tossing and turning. You just stay there until lunch. I think you'd better have soup, not the roast, if your tummy is still bad.'

Mick's protests were cut short. He had forgotten he was supposed to have an upset stomach. While Claire and Mum had a lovely meal, he sipped boiling hot, watery soup.

Offering to wash up after lunch, he licked out the pans and stuffed half a packet of biscuits into his mouth.

At last the day ended. Everything was going as planned. Emma was staying at David's parents' house, so she did not realize her money had gone. Mum had not missed anything from the cupboards. The caravan key and address were in his anorak pocket, along with all the money. Thirty-two pounds, eighty-four pence. That would last for ages.

Mick could not sleep. He was too excited. Tomorrow was going to be the biggest adventure of his life. Tomorrow Sandy would be his. He could hardly wait.

7

Mick woke up early. He was dying to get on with his plan. If he did anything differently this morning, Mum would guess that he was up to something, so he lay in bed until she had called him twice. Normal so far. Then he put his school clothes on and had an enormous breakfast. Mum did not notice his big appetite. Claire breezed in for breakfast and out the front door in her usual style.

He thought Mum would never go to work. He had not got much time, if he had to get the coach at ten-thirty. The hands on the kitchen clock seemed to have stopped, as the time was going so slowly. At last Mum went, shouting out the usual instructions.

'Do the washing-up, there's a good lad. See you at the Greers' tonight. Bye.'

Whew! She had gone. Now. Hurry!

Mick ran into his room and changed into jeans. He looked out of the window. Rainy-snow. Better put on an extra jumper and socks. Just managing to get his anorak on top, he added a scarf and thick gloves to his outfit. Now the haversack. Right. Time to go.

As casually as he could, he left the flat and walked towards school. Any nosey neighbours would think it was just an ordinary day. The sleet stung his face but he was too busy going over his plans to notice. 'Operation Sandy,' here I come!

It was ten past nine by his watch. John would be at school. Every Monday Mrs Greer went to visit her mother, after taking John to school. Her mother was ancient and did not like dogs. Sandy would be in the garage.

Mick knew where the Greers kept a spare door-key, in case they got locked out. Ah, good, it was there. He shifted the dustbin, so he could retrieve the key from the crack in the stone wall.

Carefully he let himself into the house. It was creepy. He felt as if Mr Greer was watching him, but of course he had been at work for ages by now.

Pausing to help himself to a tin of dog food, Mick picked up Sandy's lead.

'Sandy! Sandy!' he called softly, as he opened the door between the kitchen and garage.

She bounded up to him and he knelt down by her.

'Good girl,' he whispered. 'We're going on an adventure. You're mine now.'

The clasp of the lead was stiff. As he fiddled with it, he saw the guide dog medallion on Sandy's collar. He tried to break it off but it was too strong. Never mind. No-one would look at it.

At last they were ready. Mick locked the door and remembered to replace the key, exactly as he had found it. He dare not get the bus to the coach station. Someone might recognize him. So he and Sandy set off along the windy, wet paths to the station. Mick had to hurry. The minutes were zooming by.

As he queued up to get his ticket, Mick felt that everyone was looking at him.

They must know that he was running away. Someone was bound to stop him.

'Single to Rhyl,' he said.

'That dog with you?' asked the man behind the counter.

'Yes, why?' replied Mick.

'Needs a ticket,' said the man gruffly. 'That will be twelve pounds, forty-seven pence.'

Mick counted out the money. Over twelve pounds!

His money would run out at this rate.

'Where does the bus go from?' he asked.

'Platform B,' came the reply. 'Eh, not on your own, are you?'

'No, no,' lied Mick. 'Mum's over there,' he added, pointing vaguely at a group of people. 'She's seeing me on to the coach. I'm going to my gran's.'

At platform B there were loads of people. Mick hung around by them. He did not want to be asked any more awkward questions. The coach driver let them on and Mick scurried to the back dragging Sandy with him. At last everyone was settled and shouting goodbyes to people.

Mick realized with horror that the driver was working his way down the coach, checking the tickets.

'On your own?' he asked as he approached Mick. Mick had rehearsed this scene many times. He knew exactly what to say.

'Yes. I've been poorly. I'm going to my gran's. With the dog,' he added, somewhat unnecessarily as Sandy was fairly obvious.

'Where 's your mum, then? Who brought you here?' asked the driver.

'Oh, she's over there. Waving.' Mick waved at a group of people, who were waving to someone else on the coach. 'She said I was to ask you to put me off at Rhyl.'

The driver seemed convinced by his story. 'Okay, lad,' he smiled. 'Have to check, you know. Can't be responsible for runaways,' he laughed. Mick forced himself to laugh too. It was some time before he felt he could breathe normally again.

The journey seemed to last for hours. They stopped a couple of times and the driver chatted to him, while he let Sandy stretch her legs. it was hard to tell where they were going. The sleet was definitely rain now. The coach windows kept steaming up and, when Mick rubbed them with his gloves, all he could see was grey miserable countryside.

Sandy started whining. She must be hungry. Mick shared his thick wad of sandwiches with her. The tin of dog food would have to wait until he found a tin-opener at the caravan.

As they drove along, Mick began to wonder what on earth he was doing. He felt very lonely. That was strange. How could he be lonely on a coach full of noisy chattering people? Even with Sandy he felt alone. Well, he could hardly go back, could he? He pulled the caravan address out of his pocket and tried to learn it. How would he get to Bodelwyddan?

Eventually they reached Rhyl. The passengers got off. Oh, help, here was the friendly driver again.

'Now then, lad,' he began. 'Where's this gran of yours?'

'Look,' said Mick pointing. 'She's having a cup of tea in the little café. Come on, Sandy.' And he ran as fast as he could towards the café shouting 'Gran! Gran!' as convincingly as he could. When he glanced back at the driver, he was pleased to see that he had disappeared into the boot, to look for someone's suitcase.

Mick ran round the corner and stopped to catch his breath. Sandy, thinking this was some great game, jumped up and started to lick his face.

'Oh, Sandy,' Mick said, hugging her. 'Not much longer now.' He was desperate for a drink and so was Sandy. He did not dare to go into the café. There might be more awkward questions, so he found the gents loo and filled a wash basin with water. He scooped it up in his hand, until he could drink no more. Then he did the same for Sandy, splashing water all over the place.

Mick then went to where the timetables were. He needed a bus to the Bod-place. Trouble was the buses went to all sorts of funny-sounding places. He would never work out which was the right one. Deciding to take the risk, he asked a couple of people where to get the bus to Bodelwyddan. They could not understand him, so he showed them the name on his piece of paper.

'You want the number forty-eight to Abergele,' said the older woman. 'Goes right through Bodelwyddan. Catch it just over there.'

Mick and Sandy went to the bus stop and sat and waited . . . and waited. Fortunately there was a shelter, as it was still pouring down. Mick sat on his haversack, unaware that his biscuits were being crushed to crumbs, and leaned on Sandy. At last the bus came and in half an hour the tired travellers were standing on the pavement in the Bod-place. It was dark, wet and cold. Why anyone in his right mind wanted a caravan out here was beyond Mick. He shivered. All he wanted to do was to find the caravan. He did not want to ask anyone the way. Not yet. He walked one way up the road, but could find nothing. Seeing a newsagent's, he went in, bought a chocolate bar and asked the way to Green Lane. He could not wander about for ever. The newsagent told him where to go.

Following the instructions, the pair trudged through the deserted streets. Mick was soaked. His wet shoes rubbed his poor feet. The haversack weighed a ton, with the straps biting into his thin shoulders through the layers of jumpers. He had never felt so miserable in his life. At least before, when he had been so unhappy, he had been warm and comfortable. I hate Wales, he thought. I hate everyone. If they had let me have Sandy, I would not be stuck out here, in the pouring rain, looking for a stupid caravan.

Sandy obediently followed him up Green Lane. Here it was. 'Owen's Caravan Park'. All locked up. Huge gates barred the entrance. Through the wrought iron gates Mick could see all these caravans. Nearly there. He climbed the gates. 'Come on, Sandy,' he called. Sandy whined. The gates were too high to jump. Wearily Mick climbed back over.

'Come on, you great dollop,' he said. Sandy was like a lump of lead. Mick heaved like crazy, and somehow got her over the gate.

'Stay,' he commanded. Sandy sat by the haversack and Mick found his torch.

'Pen-y-bont,' he kept saying, as he walked along the deserted rows of caravans. They were shut up all right. No-one would find him here until next summer. That was ages away.

The caravans all had fancy names. 'Hill-top View', 'Summer's Edge' and loads of Welsh names that were too hard to say. At last Mick found it. 'Pen-y-bont', near the back, well away from the road. He fumbled with the key. Great, the door opened. He went to turn on the light – nothing. Suppose the electricity is turned off for the winter, he thought. Still it's my home now.

With a burst of energy, he ran to get Sandy. Even the haversack did not seem so heavy. Together the boy and his dog ran up the hill to 'Pen-y-bont'. Now he was here, Mick felt happy. Far away he could see the lights of the village. Up here he was safe. No-one around at all.

Sandy and Mick quickly explored the caravan. Thank goodness there was a Calor Gas cooker and some matches. He would be able to cook. Also there were some tins, in a cupboard, and a pile of blankets. He was too tired to do anything energetic.

Tipping the contents of his haversack onto the floor, he found the crushed biscuits and ate the lot. After a lot of attempts with a weird tin-opener, he managed to open the dog food for Sandy. She wolfed it down in seconds.

Then Mick stripped off all his wet clothes and put on his spare jumper. Heaping the blankets onto a bunk bed, he crawled into them.

‘Sandy, come here,’ he commanded. ‘Up,’ The beautiful golden dog, now bedraggled and dirty, sprang onto the bed and lay half-across him. Mick clasped his arms round her warm firm body. ‘It’s all right, girl,’ he said. ‘We’re safe here. No-one will get us.’ He glanced at his watch. Only ten past seven. It felt like midnight.

Mick was shattered. He had a headache and every bone in his body ached. It was very dark out here but he must not waste the torch batteries. He was a bit scared. If only Mum, or even his sisters, were next door, it would not be so bad. How was he going to manage on his own out here? ‘I wish I were back home,’ he sniffed. Then he remembered when he had been so unhappy at Dad’s house, he had asked Jesus to be with him then. What had Steve said? Jesus is with us everywhere. That included this cold, lonely caravan in this awful wet Welsh town.

‘Jesus, thank you that I’m not really alone,’ he said aloud. ‘Help me not to be scared. Help me, please, to look after Sandy. Thank you.’

He snuggled closer to Sandy. Worn out by the fears and excitements of the day and by trudging along the streets, he quickly fell asleep. The silence of the shadowy caravan was broken only by the mingled, shallow breathing of Mick and Sandy.

He had got her, for ever, now.

8

Mick felt very strange. There was an odd greenish-grey light in his room and something solid pinning him down into his bed. Why had he not heard Mum call him to get up? He rubbed his eyes and opened them properly. His memory came flooding back. He was not at home but in the caravan. Carefully he reached out and stroked Sandy. She grunted and woke up and began to lick his hand.

'Hi, Sandy,' Mick began. 'Let's get some food.' They rolled off the bed. It was freezing. His bare legs were covered in goose pimples. Reaching over to get his clothes, he found they were still damp, so he put his spare jeans on. It was still cold. I'll be an Indian, he thought, and attempted to wrap a blanket around himself. Ah, that felt better. Now – food.

A quick look in the cupboard revealed tins of soup and meatballs and little else. Mick decided to open his own baked beans and warm them up. However, when he tried to light the little oven, nothing happened. He could hear the gas hissing but the matches were damp.

'Oh, rats!' he said and sat down to share the cold baked beans with Sandy. Now for a drink. He turned on the tap – nothing happened.

'You stupid caravan,' he yelled and kicked the wall as hard as he could. His foot went straight through the inner plywood wall, shattering the wood and cutting his foot. That had not helped at all.

He let his foot bleed for a while and when it stopped, he rammed on his shoes.

'Let's find water, Sandy,' he said. 'Come.'

Quietly they left the caravan. It was still raining. All he could see were dingy caravans looming out of the mist. There was not a sound or any sign of anyone about. Still, he had better be quiet.

They set off exploring. It was fun really. He was the only person in the world. This whole caravan site was just for him. He soon found what he was looking for. A toilet block. It looked locked up. Well, there was only one thing to do. Taking a brick, he smashed a window, carefully removed most of the broken glass, dragged a dustbin up to the window and climbed through. It was a bit of a squeeze, but he made it. As he jumped down on the floor, he realized he had got nothing to put the water in. Why did everything take so long when you did it yourself?

Out through the window, back to 'Pen-y-bont', hunt for a bucket, back to the toilets, throw the bucket through the window, climb through the window, fill the bucket and now what? Crawling through a window with a full bucket was not easy. Most of the water got spilt but at least there was enough for Sandy to drink.

They returned to the caravan. He was soaking wet again, his shoes were caked with mud, his foot hurt, the knee had ripped out of his jeans climbing through the window and Mick was not sure what to do next. Even Sandy seemed a bit fed up. She did not like all this rain.

Mick looked round the caravan. What a home! Mud and blood-smeared. Freezing cold. Covered in wet clothes and blankets. This adventure was not turning out as he had expected. Still, Sandy was with him, but just look at her. What a mess! He could comb her and get her all clean again.

It took him the rest of the morning to tidy Sandy up. It was a good job she was so patient. Mick only had his own comb with him and it was slow work parting the tangled hair. Mick enjoyed it though. She was his dog now.

Soon his stomach told him it was lunch time. Attacking a tin of meatballs, he got it open and shared it, cold, with Sandy. It was revolting, so he ate half the chunk of cheese. He would have to do something about food. He would go shopping.

Putting Sandy on her lead, he set off. He could not face heaving her over the locked gates, so they explored along the hedge, until they found a gap big enough to squeeze through.

Down the lane they trudged. Mick did not stop to think what a sight they made. The golden, well-bred dog and the scruffy, runny-nosed boy, smeared in mud. At last the rain was stopping. He would dry out eventually.

They reached the village and shops. Mick looked around. He needed to find a small supermarket to buy food. If he went into a little grocer's shop, they might ask him questions. He found what he wanted and went inside, tying Sandy to a lamp-post outside.

It was warm, bright and clean in the shop and Mick took his time choosing his purchases. Tins were easiest, although heavy. He bought eight tins of dog food and some tinned sausages, baked beans and rice pudding for himself. A box of cornflakes, a loaf of bread, two pints of long-life milk, a comic and, oh, of course, the precious matches, completed his shopping.

'Not seen you around here before,' said the jolly woman at the cash desk.

Mick said nothing. Why did people ask questions wherever you went?

'Lost your tongue, have you?' carried on the woman, piling his things into a cardboard box.

Mick grinned at her and put on his best 'I'm stupid' face, as he paid for the goods. Perhaps she would think he was a bit simple.

He untied Sandy and counted out the rest of his money. Less than ten pounds left. It was not going to last long. Then what would he do? He would just have to eat the meatballs back at the caravan.

Slowly they returned home. The box of food was awkward and heavy to carry. Mick kept stopping for a rest. His nose was running and he still ached all over. After a long time they were back at the caravan. Mick lit the gas ring to try to warm the place up. It did not do much but looked bright and cheerful. After unpacking the food, he decided it was time for tea.

Tipping the sausages and beans into a pan, he left them to warm, while he fed Sandy. She was pleased to have her proper food again and licked up every bit. By the time Mick had fed her, the sausages and beans had warmed up all right. They were stuck solid to the sides and bottom of the pan. Undeterred, Mick attacked them with a spoon. At least they were hot!

As he sat with the warm pan on his knee, scraping off the burned bits with a knife and chewing them slowly, he wondered what would happen next. He had believed that once he had Sandy he would be happy. Well, he had got her now. There she was, lying fast asleep across his feet, keeping him warm. But was he happy? Not much. It was not so great eating burned food, hiding away from people and crawling through a window every time he wanted a drink. It would have been good fun with his mates, though. He and John would have had a right laugh. But his mates were not here. He was on his own. There was no one to have a laugh with. No one to join in his adventure. There was only Sandy.

He stared down at her. Perhaps it was worth it after all. He knew that she loved him and he loved her so much. He could tell her just how he felt.

'Sandy,' he said out loud. 'What are we going to do

next?' He paused. Trouble was, Sandy could not talk back. 'We're stuck,' Mick continued. 'I don't think I like it here, but there isn't anywhere else to go. I daren't go home. They'll kill me. And anyway,' he added practically, 'I haven't got enough money for the coach fare.' He sat there for a long time, thoughts chasing around in his head.

It was dark by now. He might as well go to sleep. He felt awful. His clothes were still damp, his sock had stuck into the cut on his foot and he was sneezing all the time. Crawling under the pile of blankets, he snuggled up to Sandy, just as he had the night before.

'Oh, God,' he cried. 'What am I going to do?' He tried to think of nice things to make him feel happy. Like warm beds, one of Mrs Greer's dinners, his holiday with Dad, but that just made it worse. He could not sleep as his foot was throbbing too much. Why had things not worked out? Why did he not feel happy now? He had been sure his plan to 'Get Sandy' was great but now he felt it was just another disappointment.

As tiredness started to take over, he remembered a Bible story they had been told one week at church. A lamb had got lost and the shepherd had hunted everywhere until he found it. He was a bit like the lamb. He was not exactly lost. He knew he was in the Bod-place. But he felt lost. He felt like he wanted to be found. He wanted to be cared for by the shepherd. That was Jesus.

'Please, Jesus, find me,' he asked. 'I want to go home, but I can't. Please get me found . . . and let me keep Sandy,' he added as he drifted off to sleep.

9

While Mick slept fitfully, tossing and turning, dreaming of cold meatballs and rainy Welsh countryside, his prayers were being answered. If only he had known what had been going on back at home!

No-one had realized anything was wrong until Monday evening.

'Where's Mick?' asked Mrs Greer, when John came out of school on his own.

'Not here today,' replied John briefly. 'Must be ill.'

Mrs Greer was cross. 'Well, his Mum should have let me know. I've got enough to worry about.'

'What's up?' asked John. Mum looked really worked up and tense. Usually she was quite calm.

'It's Sandy,' Mrs Greer said. 'She's gone.'

'What, already?' asked John. 'I thought the Guide Dog people were fetching her tomorrow.'

'Not that sort of gone,' replied his mum. 'She's lost, disappeared, vanished. I got back from Grandma's after lunch and there was no sign of her. I can't understand it. I'm sure I left her in the garage.'

'Where is she?' asked John, rather pointlessly.

'I don't know. Aren't you listening?' snapped his mum. 'I've walked miles looking for her. Dad's coming home early to drive round and see if she'll turn up.'

John fell silent. He knew Sandy had to go, but not like this. He would miss her, he knew, but there would be the new puppy, Ben, to play with. As they got home, Dad arrived. John went with him to drive around the area.

'You will have to phone the Guide Dog people,' he shouted, as he drove off. 'Tell them what has happened.'

Mrs Greer made the phone call and then rang the police to tell them of the missing dog. She was tired and sat down with a cup of tea. In next to no time she had nodded off. The loud ringing of the doorbell woke Mrs Greer with a start. Still feeling dozy, she staggered to the door.

'Oh, it's you,' she said to Mrs Browning. 'Come to apologize, I suppose?'

'Apologize! What for?'

'Look here, I don't mind having Mick but you could have let me know he was off school. I don't like being messed about.' Mrs Greer, worried about Sandy, was cross at Mick's mum.

'Off school? Course he's not off school. I've just come to collect him, like normal.'

Mrs Greer looked straight at Mrs Browning. Slowly she was putting two and two together.

'Sorry,' she said more kindly. 'You'd better come in.'

The two women brewed another pot of tea and talked for a long time. A missing dog, a missing boy. The boy loved the dog. They must be together. Mrs Greer looked and found that the lead was missing.

'They are together, I'm sure,' said Mrs Browning. 'He's potty about that dog.'

'But where?' asked Mrs Greer. 'I've looked everywhere. We'll have to phone the police again.'

'I'd better get home,' said Mrs Browning. 'He might be there.' She thought it unlikely but it was best to make sure. No point in phoning the police, if he had just played truant at home all day.

Emma was at home and in a foul mood. Not noticing how worn and strained her mother looked, she launched immediately into a flood of words.

'Who's had it?' she demanded. 'Twenty pounds gone.

I've told you not to borrow it. Twenty pounds!' She paused. 'What's up, Mum?'

'It's Mick. Is he here?'

'No, I thought you collected him on the way home.'

'I didn't think he would be here. He's run away with that hulk of a dog belonging to the Greers. Run over and tell them he's not here. I'll phone the police.' For once, Emma obeyed, saying nothing. Mum went to the public phone box and tried to explain what had happened. A few minutes later a police car pulled up. Half the neighbours chose to watch what was happening but Mrs Browning was past caring.

The policeman and woman asked her lots of questions about where he was likely to be. The Greers arrived with Emma, all talking at once. John thought it was very exciting. Fancy Mick running away with Sandy! He never thought he had it in him. He would be able to tell all their mates about it at school – perhaps even get a ride in a police-car, with sirens wailing! His thoughts were interrupted. The policeman was talking to him. No, he did not not know that Mick was going to run away. No, he did not know where he was.

By now Mrs Browning was crying. The policeman told her to work out what clothes Mick had been wearing and to find a photograph.

In his bedroom, Mrs Browning saw the discarded heap of school clothes and discovered which jumpers and jeans were missing. The only recent photo was a school one. Hair cut and shiny clean face, shirt buttoned up correctly, it did not look much like Mick at all, but the policeman took it willingly.

'Now, don't worry,' he said. Not that anyone stopped worrying. 'He's probably holed up in a shed somewhere on the estate, or in one of the empty garages. I'll leave WPC Jones with you, Mrs Browning. We'll get looking. Pity it's dark.'

'But he's got my money,' butted in Emma. 'He could be anywhere.'

'I know,' said Sergeant Tring quietly.

Mr Greer said he would organize some search volunteers and soon a band of men and police were searching the area. Emma had phoned Claire, who was staying late at college, and they too joined the search.

They found nothing. At midnight Sergeant Tring returned to the flat, wet from searching in the rain.

'We'll resume the search at first light,' he said, water dripping from his raincoat all over the carpet. 'He'll be safe somewhere. Now I want you to get some sleep and try to think where he might have gone to. His dad's?'

'No,' said Mrs Browning. 'I phoned him. He's driving up to help us look.'

'Well, there's no more we can do tonight,' he said. 'I'll be back in the morning.'

Next morning Sergeant Tring arrived at nine o'clock.

'We've been looking for a couple of hours,' he said. 'No luck so far. Now I want you all to think really hard. Has Mick done anything unusual the last couple of days? Anything out of the ordinary that might give us a clue to his whereabouts?'

He looked around the room at the families. Mrs Browning looked as if she had not slept a wink. Claire and Emma looked little better, although Claire had found the energy to put on a thick layer of dark eye make-up. Mrs Greer was making more tea, and that boy, John, looked like he was enjoying every minute. Somehow no-one had thought to make him go off to school. He had already listened to the local radio news bulletins three times. 'Boy and dog missing.' His best friend and his dog. Made him feel quite important.

Claire broke the silence.

'He spent hours at the library on Saturday,' she said. 'Usually he forgets to take his books back on time and they weren't even due back yet. I know because I got some books out last time with him.'

'Well, I'll ask some questions over there, I think,' said Sergeant Tring, as no-one else had any further suggestions.

And so it was that Sergeant Tring had a most helpful conversation with the librarian and the old, newspaper-reading man. He came to the library every day. Gradually Sergeant Tring pieced together the story. A label with an address, a big key, looking up a Welsh village beginning with Bod . . . a charabanc (coach to you, young man), talking about day trips to Rhyl . . .

When Sergeant Tring returned to the Brownings' flat, he told them what he had found out.

' "Pen-y-bont"!' exclaimed Mrs Greer, who had decided she needed to stay and keep Mick's mum company.

'Pardon, Madam?' said Sergeant Tring.

' "Pen-y-bont",' she repeated. 'The caravan!'

'Caravan?' queried the policeman. Sometimes getting information from the general public could be very trying.

Mrs Greer turned to face the young sergeant. 'We have a caravan,' she said slowly, as if speaking to a five-year-old. 'It is at Bodelwyddan. Near Rhyl.' She paused. 'Mick knows we have a caravan. It's locked up for the winter. How he knew it was at Bodelwyddan, I don't know,'

'I do,' Mr Greer had just come in with Mick's dad. They had been searching for a couple of hours ever since Mr Browning had arrived. 'The crafty little so-and-so,' he said and he told the story of Mick's strange visit for the missing pen on Saturday.

'Couldn't wait to get me out of the kitchen. Bet the key's gone.'

Sergeant Tring went with him to check. The key had gone.

Dad was all for rushing off to Wales that minute. Sergeant Tring calmed him down and took him to the Police Station to make enquiries. It was early afternoon now and it would take a few hours to get to Wales. No point rushing off on a wild goose chase.

The enquiries took an age. Eventually Sergeant Tring got a report from a local Welsh policeman. Signs of a boy and dog at Owen's Caravan Park. He had peered through Pen-y-bont's windows. No-one there but clothes all over the place. He would stay hidden and watch.

After some discussion, they decided that Sergeant Tring would drive Dad to Wales. They were concerned that Mick would be frightened, or just run off, if the Welsh policeman approached him. He would let them know if and when Mick returned.

A couple of hours later, as darkness fell, the Welsh policeman was able to report to Sergeant Tring's patrol car: 'Boy and dog entering "Pen-y-bont". Boy carrying box of groceries. Limping. Otherwise well.'

As Mick lay tossing and turning under his pile of blankets, help was speeding towards him. As he prayed to be found, Dad was only thirty miles away. The Welsh policeman was keeping watch. Rescue was near at hand. But what would happen when he was found? How was he going to get out of this mess?

10

By the next afternoon, Mick knew that he was in a mess.

It had been marvellous when Dad and what seemed like a posse of policeman had raided the caravan. Dad had woken him gently. Mick was so exhausted, he had not heard him enter the caravan or felt Sandy leap off the bed, growling at these invaders in her territory.

'Mick, Mick,' Dad shook him gently and then more firmly. Mick was in the middle of a dream. A giant meatball was rolling down a hill towards him. He had got to get out of the way. He was trapped. He could feel the earth shaking. He woke with a jerk. He was shaking. Sitting bolt upright, he felt strong arms around him and heard Dad, yes Dad, of all people, saying 'It's all right, Mick,' over and over again. Dad helped him change into a clean set of clothes. Mick was so happy, though he felt dreadful, shivering all over.

'Running a temperature, I should think. Daft beggar, choosing January to run away in.' Some strange voice reached his ears.

He remembered little of the journey home, as he kept falling asleep. Dad and the policeman were talking, about him mostly, but it did not make sense. Dad was with him and Sandy in the back of the car as they sped through the night. He had got to stay awake. A long, fast ride, in a police car. He would be a right wally to fall asleep. But no matter how hard he tried, he dozed off.

'I'm found,' he suddenly said, between dozes. 'I'm found.' Dad smiled at him.

'You certainly are. No getting lost again, eh?'

'No, Dad. Can we have the siren on?'

Sergeant Tring explained that sirens were for emergencies, not for taking boy runaways back home. After that, Mick kept silent.

When he got home, Mum and all the Greer family were there, which was funny as it was the middle of the night. Mum took one look at him and burst into tears. At this, Claire and Emma joined in and then Mrs Greer started. What a racket! What were they crying for?

Mick was bundled off to bed, dosed with tablets for 'flu and, wonder of wonders, Sandy was allowed to sleep in his room. In the morning he was told to stay in bed. He did not mind, he felt dreadful. Now it was afternoon and Dad had just come in.

'Time for a talk,' he said.

Mick groaned inwardly. This was it. Trouble. Everyone had been too nice to him so far. Better keep quiet.

'First, you've got 'flu. Got to stay in bed. Mum has taken the rest of the week off work.' Dad paused. How was he going to get through the next bit? He would keep the worst part until last.

'Second,' he continued, 'no pocket money until after Easter, to help pay back the money you took from Emma and Mum.' So Mum had found the electricity money had gone.

'And third,' Dad paused for along time. He shifted his gaze from Mick's pale, but clean, face and seemed fascinated by the jet fighter poster near his head. 'And third,' he repeated, 'Sandy's gone. For good. The Guide Dog people came for her at lunchtime. Fortunately for you she's not injured. Valuable dog like that. Could have cost us a fortune if she had been damaged.' Dad was talking too much now. Mick was not listening. 'Sandy's gone.' No! No! he screamed inside. I can't bear it! He did not notice Dad leave the room. Sandy! Gone! I didn't even say goodbye, he thought. He reach out his arm automatically, just as he had at the caravan. No Sandy to pat, to stroke, to love. Gone. For ever.

He rolled over on his stomach and started to cry. Great tears dripped down his face soaking his pillow. Sobs shook his body. 'No, no,' he cried aloud, his heart breaking. This was terrible. Worse even than Dad leaving home. At least he still saw Dad. He would never see Sandy again. Not ever.

His head pounded with crying. Making a supreme effort, he tried to pull himself together. He blew his nose, like a trumpet, on the only thing available, the sheet, and rolled over again onto his back. He lay there for what seemed like ages, wrapped in his misery. He would never love another dog again. Never.

'It's your fault, God,' he said, looking at the patch on the wall where his 'Get Sandy' prayer had been stuck up for so long. 'I asked for Sandy but you didn't give her to me. Why? Why?' He clenched his fists tightly under the bedclothes. 'Okay,' he carried on. 'You got me found . . . Thanks . . . But Sandy . . .' His voice tailed off and he sniffed loudly. 'How could you? I learned the verse.' He quoted, ' "You do not have what you want because you do not ask God for it." I asked and asked. Why didn't you give her to me? Why? I'll never ask you for anything again. There's no point.' In his anger and sadness, Mick pounded the bed with his fists and kicked at the wall with his feet. It did not help. Nothing helped. Nothing would bring Sandy back.

Mum brought him some tea but he did not feel like eating. She sat quietly with him until he fell asleep. The 'flu tablets and his sorrow had left him exhausted and he slept until morning.

Next day Dad went back to his home and Mick stayed in bed. It was really boring. John came to visit after school. He rattled on and on about how he had told everyone at school what had happened. How he gave the police the vital clue to Mick's whereabouts. This was news to Mick. It would have been news to Sergeant Tring as well! He gave Mick a blow by blow account of what had happened with lots of 'he said this' and 'I did that' in it.

Mick listened half-heartedly. John had enjoyed Mick's great escape. That was more than Mick had done, although he managed to make the story of the coach journey sound quite exciting.

'Time to go,' Mrs Greer's voice came through the door. 'Five more minutes, John.'

'I've got you a present,' said John and dug deep into his school bag. 'You're not to open it until I've gone, Mum said. And here's some sweets. Can I have some?' Without waiting for an answer, he unwrapped a chocolate bar and stuffed it into his mouth. Mick tried to grab it from him, missed and fell out of bed. John dived on top of him and the two boys were just enjoying a friendly scrap when their mums came in, separated them, and tucked the reluctant invalid back into bed. Mick smiled. John was okay really.

After John had gone, Mick remembered the present. It had got tucked into the bedclothes somehow. What could it be? It was a flat, hard, square parcel. Mick tore the wrapping paper off it. A frame with a photograph in it. Sandy. The soft brown eyes seemed to be looking straight at him. He had no tears left now. Just a hollow feeling inside. A hole filled with sadness. Gently he kissed the photograph.

'I'll never forget you,' he said. He sat looking at her for ages. He would hide the photograph, so no-one else could see it, and just look at it in private. Putting it under his socks in the drawer, he stretched and thought. Mum was always talking about 'making the best of it'. I suppose I'll have to do that, he thought, although it seemed so unfair.

The rest of the week passed slowly. John came to play a lot. That was fun, otherwise it was boring at home. He watched some ancient films on television, got in Mum's way and decided that even going back to school was something to look forward to.

On Sunday, Mum left Claire in charge and went to church as usual. Mick, although much better, said he did not feel well enough to go. Mum eyed him with suspicion. Last time she had left him, he had planned his escape. Was that only a week ago? Telling Claire to watch him like a hawk, she went off. Mick was very surprised when she came home with Steve, his Sunday School teacher.

Steve had dinner with them and then told Mick he would teach him to play chess. Mick found the rules complicated. As soon as he worked out where to move one piece, he had to learn how to move the next.

'I'm fed up with this,' he said, giving the chessboard a shove, which resulted in the kings and queens toppling over.

'So, I see,' smiled Steve. 'What's the matter?'

'Nothing,' replied Mick and became silent.

'Your mum says you have been fed up since you came home,' said Steve. 'Do you still feel ill?'

'No!' exclaimed Mick. 'It's just not fair. He didn't take any notice when I asked. I'm not asking again.'

'Who didn't? What are you talking about?' Steve was puzzled.

'Your mate. You know. Him up there – God!'

'God?' queried Steve. 'What's he done?'

'Nothing. Nothing at all. That's the trouble. He didn't do anything!' Mick's voice went quieter.

'What did you want him to do?'

Really, Mick thought, Steve was fine as adults went, but surely he knew the answer to his own question. He jumped up and began to pace up and down the room like a caged tiger.

'Give me Sandy, of course,' he said. 'What did you think?'

'Well, I kind of guessed it might be that,' replied Steve. 'Now you're cross at him because he did not do what you asked.'

'Too right I am,' said Mick. 'It's the vicar's fault. He kept telling us to ask God for things and we'd get them. Well, he's a liar, that's for sure.'

Steve sat calmly. 'What else did the vicar say?' he asked. 'Can you remember?'

Mick told him the stories ending with the dog Spot getting better. 'Why didn't he answer my prayers?' he asked. 'Why?'

'Have you got the Bible I gave you when you started to come to church?' Mick nodded. 'Go and fetch it, please.'

Mick disappeared and, after five minutes, found it propping up his wobbly desk leg. He had not bothered reading it since it became obvious that God was not going to help him to get Sandy. He gave it to Steve.

'Ah, here. James chapter 4. See you've marked it.' Steve pointed to the old brown toffee smear. 'Will you read it to me? Verse three.'

' "You do not have what you want because you do not ask God for it." ' Mick gabbled and stopped.

'Go on,' said Steve gently. 'The next bit as well.'

Mick was getting fed up with this. I bet Mum has made him come to talk to me, he thought. Mum had conveniently found something to do elsewhere. He sighed, took a deep breath and carried on. ' "And when you ask, you do not receive it, because your motives are bad; you ask for things to use for your own pleasures." ' He shut the Bible.

'Well, there you are,' stated Steve. What was he on

about? thought Mick. He said nothing.

Steve was not deterred. 'Sandy was never right for you, Mick. She's for a blind person. If God had given her to you, what would the blind person have done?' Have another dog, thought Mick, but did not say so. 'You wanted Sandy for yourself. That was selfish, Mick. Do you understand?'

'No,' replied Mick bluntly. How could it be selfish to want Sandy? These grown-ups always had an answer for everything.

Steve looked at him. He was getting nowhere. 'I'll pray that you'll understand,' he said.

'Okay,' said Mick. Do what you like, he thought. It makes no difference.

Selfish! Steve didn't understand. He had had enough of this conversation.

'Show me how the bishops move again, will you please?' he said, changing the subject. Steve straightened the board and carried on teaching Mick to play chess. At the back of Mick's mind a little jingle was going non-stop. It was like a tongue-twister. 'Selfish – Sandy, Sandy – Selfish.' I'll never believe that, thought Mick. It's stupid. He added the word to his tongue-twister. Sandy, selfish, stupid. It was jolly hard to say and he grinned to himself. Even harder to believe Steve. He would try that. Sandy, selfish, stupid Steve! That's better. Steve was stupid all right.

11

Winter went on for ever. One boring day after another – school, John's house, home, television, bed – what a drag! Mick was fed up. He never mentioned Sandy, or much else really. He had decided it was pointless to want things, or to tell people how he felt. No-one listened to him, no-one bothered.

The winter half-term was a bit different. Mick went to stay at Dad's and met Philip for the first time. Philip was the new baby – very new. He cried or slept and did little else. Dad was too busy to take Mick out, and Pamela was too tired. At night Mick would hear Philip crying and lights would go on, as Pamela got up to feed him.

One day Pamela approached him.

'Do you want to hold your little half-brother?' she asked.

Mick thought it best to say yes. He sat down carefully on the sofa and watched the tiny bundle on his knee. Half-brother indeed. That's what he was. No good for playing football with for years. Yet, as he watched the tiny face crumple and wrinkle, Mick felt a strange tenderness. Okay, Philip was a bit boring now, but when he was older he could teach him to build dens, play cricket, go swimming. Gently he put his own grubby finger into the baby's clenched fist and felt Philip grip on to him. 'Okay, kid,' he said in his best cowboy voice. 'You and me will get along fine, see. We'll be mates.' He sat there quietly imagining all the fun they would have. Suddenly there was a rumbling noise. It came from the baby who squirmed, made a rude sound and shot a stream of brown goo right down Mick's trousers.

'Pamela! Pamela!' he yelled. She rushed into the room, took one look and burst out laughing. Mick was not amused. Pamela retrieved the baby, cleaned Mick up and sent him to get changed. By the time Dad came home that night and Pamela told him the story, Mick laughed as much as the others. Perhaps having a half-brother might not be so bad as he had thought. None of his mates had got one. He could tell stories of Philip and make them laugh.

Only one other thing broke the monotony of those winter days. Well not exactly a thing. A 'he'. Ben. The black labrador puppy that was now resident at the Greers' house.

He could not have been more different from Sandy. He was jet black, with slightly curly hair, and quite timid to start with. He was a terror at chewing things. One day Mick got to John's house to find that Ben was in disgrace. So was John. John had left the fridge door open and Ben had investigated. He had eaten the meat for the evening meal, left paw marks in the butter, hairs on the cheese, broken some eggs and licked out a whole carton of cream. The effect of all this on a tiny pup was to make him very sick. In the ironing basket. On top of the clean laundry.

John was banished to his room, Ben was locked in the garage and Mrs Greer had a horrible mess to clear up. Mick wisely decided to keep out of her way and found an old comic stuffed under a chair to read.

He had a problem with Ben. He had promised himself never to love another dog. Never. Yet sometimes he wanted so much to join in the fun with Ben. To play catch the ball, to charge around the garden. To sit with him falling asleep on his knee. Yet he could not. He must not. He had promised the photo of Sandy, only last night, never to love Ben or any other dog.

John and his parents did not help. Always going on. 'Come and join in.' 'Would you like to feed him, take him for a walk?' He could hear them whispering about him trying to make him get involved, trying to help him to 'get over Sandy'. Well, he did not want to get over Sandy. Sometimes he had to think very hard to remember just what she looked like. Then he would get his photo from his drawer and attempt to memorize her face. If he played with Ben, he would be disloyal to Sandy. Anyway Ben would have to go to the Guide Dog people just like Sandy did. No way was he going to love something again and have it taken from him. He heard his mum come in. Mrs Greer was telling her what Ben had done. Mick put his ear by the wall to listen.

'. . . and Mick said nothing. Did not laugh or comment,' Mrs Greer was talking. 'He's changed so much. No trouble, don't get me wrong, but no life in him. He will not join in.'

'I know.' That was Mum. 'Worries me to death, he does. It's ever since he ran away. I'd even let him have a dog now if we lived somewhere suitable. He just can't accept what's happened. My only hope is that he'll grow out of it, get over it in time.' She was coming towards the living room. Mick moved at the speed of light, away from his listening post, and was sitting innocently in his chair when Mum came in.

On the way home Mick had a new thought. Mum had said she was worried about him. The Greers kept talking to him. Perhaps they thought he was somebody after all. If they were worried about him then he must be important. Right, I will keep them worrying. I will not play with Ben, even when I really want to, he thought. Strangely he felt happier than he had for ages. He was important. They did care about him!

It was very hard to keep to his promise but Mick

worked out a way of doing it. To stop Mrs Greer going on and on, he and John played happily after school. Now the weather was getting better, they could practise football a lot. However, he would not play with Ben. Well, not if anyone else was around. Sometimes he would find Ben when everyone else was busy. Ben loved to roll on his back, feet in the air and have his tummy tickled. He would squirm with delight and Mick loved tickling him.

One night all the Greers were busy and Mick had taken Ben into the garage to play their usual game.

'Hey. Great to see you having fun.' Mick whirled round. Mr Greer! Creeping up on him. Spying!

'What you doing?' he demanded.

'Only come to get a light bulb. The one in the hall has gone out,' Mr Greer explained.

'You are spying on me. Following me,' Mick said.

'Don't be so daft.' Mr Greer went to pat him on the shoulder but Mick dodged out of the way. Ben was behind him. He tripped and went flying, banging his head on the door. Hurt and angry at being found playing with Ben, Mick lashed out.

'Why can't you all leave me alone? I know you talk about me. I've heard you. Just lay off, will you?' He pushed past Mr Greer and ran out of the house and all the way home to the flat.

As he sat on the cold doorstep getting his breath back, he felt cross. Mum, he knew, would send him back to apologize. He would probably get a good hiding. They would not worry about him any more. They would not care.

He was right about the first two things. After the good hiding and the apologizing, which was worse, Mum had sat him down in a chair.

'Now, listen,' she began. Mick had not much choice. She was shouting. She always shouted when she was upset or angry. Today she was both. 'I've had enough of your stupid behaviour. What are you trying to prove? It's not my fault, the Greers' fault, anybody's fault, that Sandy had to go. Stop punishing yourself and everyone else. You're just making us all miserable . . . and I love you Mick, I don't want to see you miserable.' Mum ran out of words but not for long. 'Look, I know you've been sad,' she carried on. 'Remember what we prayed about after Dad went? Making the best of it. Well, it seems to me you're making the worst of it! What do you think?' She sat down and stared at him.

What did he think? This was too confusing for words.

'Dunno.'

'Don't know?' Mum did not believe him. Mick thought, I suppose I have been a right pain. I did not realize how upset Mum would be. She does love me. I am important to her. Now look at her. The crossness had gone and she looked tired and old, much too old.

Mick got up. 'Oh, Mum, I'm sorry. I thought no-one bothered about what I did. No-one bothered when I wanted Sandy so much. I thought you didn't love me.'

Mum put her arms round him. 'Mick, you daft thing,' she said kindly. 'I love you all the world.' They stayed like that for a few minutes. 'Shall I pray for us?' suggested Mum. Mick nodded.

'Please Jesus, help Mick to know how much we love him. Help him to make the best of it, about Sandy.' Mum paused, 'And can you please help him to understand why he could never have her. Amen.'

'Amen,' Mick said. That meant the prayer had ended and he meant the words as well. Steve had told him that. Well, he did mean it. Some of it. I don't think I'll ever understand, he thought, but I'll make the best of it. I really will.

12

Making the best of it got easier as the days went by. In September John and Mick would be in the top class at school. Mick said he was too old to be looked after by the Greers. He could have his own key and see to himself. He did not want his mates to think he was a baby, having to be looked after.

Mum put her foot down. She would be happier with him at the Greers. She knew what he was up to there. Anyway it was company for John.

Mick did not mind really. He was a lot happier now. Every so often he felt a twinge of pain when he thought about Sandy but he no longer looked the other way whenever he saw a golden retriever like her.

However, Mick was still determined not to let himself love Ben. He played with him and took him out and allowed himself to enjoy the growing puppy. But he would not love him. That was until one day when something happened to change his mind.

It was a glorious August day. Mick had not long come back from staying at his dad's. He had had a great time but had also been reminded of last year. The promise of a dog; the promise that was broken. Now he and John were taking Ben off to the park. John wanted to go down by the stream on the way back and Mick agreed.

'We'll get Ben to play catch with us, over the stream,' John explained. 'You stay this side and me and Ben will go over there.' He pointed to a stony ridge that stuck out into the other side of the stream.

'Okay,' agreed Mick. He flicked the ball across the

water. It bounced and Ben caught it on the rebound and dashed off into the bushes with it. John chased him and eventually wrestled it off him. He lobbed it back to Mick. Every time Ben caught it, he ran off.

'Stupid dog,' thought Mick. Sandy had always brought the ball straight back when he had called her. That Ben was thick. It was all right for John. He could chase him and roll around on the grass playing. Mick, meanwhile, played the dummy, hanging around waiting for the ball to come back. He grinned. He would show the pair of them he was not such a dummy after all. And have a good laugh.

Mick aimed the ball carefully. Just at the spot where the stream tumbled down a small weir. Right in the middle of the water. Ben leaped straight into the water chasing the ball, over the rocks as it bobbed along just out of reach.

'What did you do that for?' shouted John. 'We'll lose the ball. Fetch it.'

'Fetch it yourself,' yelled Mick and sat on the grass to watch the fun.

John ripped off his trainers and paddled into the stream. It was only shallow but John was a bit clumsy. He lost his balance and, after tottering like a clown, he finally fell, face first into the water.

Mick howled with laughter. Ben had turned round and thought it was a new game. He was jumping on John, trying to lick him. They were both soaked.

'Get off, you dozy animal,' screeched John. 'You wait, I'll get even with you,' he shouted at Mick. Mick did not bother to reply. He was helpless with laughter.

John lumbered to his feet, grabbed Ben's collar and tried to drag him to Mick's side of the bank.

'I will get you. You stupid idiot.' He was so cross it made Mick laugh even more. 'You will be sorry you were born.' He tugged Ben's collar. 'Move, you animal, move.'

Ben suddenly started howling. It was an ear-splitting racket. John let go of him and spluttered to the side. 'Shut up,' he yelled. But Ben did not shut up. He carried on and did not move. 'Shut up,' he commanded again. Ben stopped and changed the howl to a pitiful whine.

'What's up?' asked Mick.

'I don't know,' said John, forgetting briefly his urge to get even with Mick, by chucking him in the water. 'Oh no!' He gasped and pointed. Near Ben the murky stream water was changing. It was going red. Blood.

'Look what you've done,' he hissed at Mick. 'You'll have to help.'

Mick was only too willing. The boys went back in the water and half-pushed, half-dragged the unfortunate dog to the bank.

It was dreadful. Ben's front right foot was hanging all wrong. Blood was pouring out of a cut, dripping all over the grass. Ben was whining more quietly now, looking puzzled at his injured leg.

'Glass,' said John. 'You idiot. There must have been glass in the stream. What are we going to do?'

'Run home and get your mum.' Mick took charge. 'Go on. Get moving, you lump,' as John hesitated before setting off, spraying water everywhere from his sodden clothes.

Mick pulled his T-shirt off. 'Lie down, Ben,' he said. Ben obeyed and Mick wrapped the T-shirt as tightly as he could round the damaged limb.

'Oh, Ben, Ben, I'm so sorry,' he said and started to cry. 'It's my fault. I threw the ball on purpose. Oh Ben, please don't die. Don't bleed to death!' The T-shirt was already heavily stained with blood and Ben was trying to chew at it.

'No leave it, there's a good boy.' Gently Mick stroked him, watching anxiously for signs of Mrs Greer's arrival.

He looked around for help but that part of the park was deserted. The blood was coming through the material now. Mick clenched his hands tightly above the cut, trying desperately to stop the blood. Where was Mrs Greer? Please God, get her here quickly.

In the distance he heard a noise and then saw a sight that, in any other circumstance, would have had him smiling. Mrs Greer's bright red Mini was bouncing and jolting over the park. Straight over the grass and along the edge of the stream. The park-keeper would have a fit. She screeched to a stop in a way that any racing driver would have been proud of.

'Get in,' she said solemnly. The look in her eyes made Mick move fast. He had better keep quiet. She had folded the back seats down. John was crouched there. He had taken his wet clothes off and was finishing putting a clean T-shirt on back to front.

Mrs Greer wrapped Ben in a tartan rug and gently put him into the car.

'Do the ice,' she commanded and jumped in and drove off, bumping and banging over the ruts. Mick stared glumly out of the back window. You could see the tyre marks on the grass but Mrs Greer was not bothered.

'What are you doing?' he whispered to John.

'Ice – round his leg. Here, help me.' John passed him a tray of ice-cubes. 'Put them in this plastic bag, on his leg. I'll do the meat.'

'The meat?' John did not reply. He was putting small packets of frozen mince and sausages round Ben's leg. Mick added his nearly melted ice-cubes.

'What's this for?' he asked again.

'I told Mum what had happened. She dived in the freezer and came out with this lot and yelled at me to find some dry clothes.'

Mrs Greer overheard them. 'It might help to stop the bleeding – the coldness.' She was driving like a lunatic.

Way above the speed limit. Normally she crawled along at one mile under the speed limit. Was this the same driver? Tooting her horn, going round corners like mad.

She slammed on the brakes and swerved into a driveway.

'Out!' Picking up Ben she rushed into the vet's, leaving Mick and John to follow her. Through the entrance, then another door, then down a corridor, another door and . . . a woman stopped them.

'Now then – what are you two doing?'

'It's Ben,' said John, pointing to the trail of bloodstains which led to yet another door.

'Well, sit down. You can't go in there. That's the surgery.'

The two boys sat down. What a sight! John still damp. Mick without a t-shirt and smeared in blood. He had wiped his tears away at the Mini's approach, rubbing blood and mud on his face.

'What will happen?' he asked John.

'Dunno. Perhaps he'll die.'

The waiting room felt cold after the heat outside. No-one else was there, except the woman who had stopped them. She was writing something behind a counter that said 'Receptionist'. After the clock on the wall had shown that five minutes had ticked slowly by, Mick got up all his courage.

'Please, miss, what's happening to Ben?'

She smiled. 'He is with the vet. Mr Poplar is very good. Now just wait quietly. You mum will be out of the surgery soon.'

They waited . . . and waited. The far door flew open. Mrs Greer came out carrying a collar and lead. But no Ben. She looked upset.

John ran to her. 'Is he dead?' he asked bluntly.

Mrs Greer turned to the boys. She had half forgotten they were here. It had been awful when the vet had shown her the cut. Ben's leg was nearly cut into two.

'No. No.' She tried to reassure the boys. 'He is having an operation. He's asleep now. Can't feel a thing. Mr Poplar is sewing his leg back . . .' She quickly changed her words. 'Sewing his leg – the cut. We've got to leave him here.'

'Can I see him?' asked Mick. He must ask Ben to forgive him. His heart was bursting with love for him and sorrow at causing the accident. The old Mick was back! The one who loved and cared, got hurt but also knew what it was to be happy.

'No, love,' said Mrs Greer kindly. 'Now let's get back home. You look a mess.'

'So do you,' pointed out John. Her summer dress was spattered with blood.

They drove home silently. Mrs Greer, the racing driver, was replaced by Mrs Greer the cautious, slow driver. As they rode along Mick turned his thoughts to prayer. He could not ask Ben to forgive him but he could ask God. 'I'm sorry,' he said in his head. 'Please forgive me for being horrid to Ben and John. Sorry, too, for not talking to you much since Sandy went away. Please be my friend again. Please let Ben be all right. Amen.' He said the 'Amen' again just to let God know that this was certainly one prayer that he really meant with all his heart.

13

Ben had to stay at the vet's for a few days. Mr Poplar wanted to keep an eye on him. He had told Mrs Greer that he might have to remove the lower leg altogether. She was very worried. Not only would that be awful for Ben but he could never be a guide dog.

Fortunately Mick and John did not realize how bad the injury was. They wanted him home. Mick knew now that he loved him. Oh, not in the same way as Sandy. No-one would ever take her place. He found, too, that it was much easier to talk to God. He had even asked John if they could pray together for Ben. John was surprised. Anything was worth a try, so he agreed. In fact, one of these Sundays he might go to church with Mick. See what it was all about.

Mick was not sure what it was all about himself! But now he knew God was his friend. Jesus was on his side. That made him feel good inside. He still had a big problem though about what Steve had said. All that stuff about wanting Sandy for himself being selfish. That would never make sense.

Ben came home the day before school started. He looked thinner and his leg was in an enormous plaster cast. He was not to walk on it. That was easier said than done.

'How ever are we going to stop him walking on it?' asked Mrs Greer. She and the boys spent the rest of the day stopping Ben walking. It was exhausting.

By the next day, Ben had solved the problem himself. When the boys went back to John's house after school, he rushed to meet them. On three legs. He looked so funny. The boys had a bet to see when he would topple over but he never did.

The plaster had to stay on for a month. Then there was another operation, more plaster until finally they all heard the great news, 'His leg is saved!' Now, with only a bandage to get in his way, Ben could charge around the house, still on three legs.

One afternoon Mrs Greer met the boys after school, this was unusual. They walked home on their own nowadays.

'Hop in!' she said, opening the car door. Ben was in the back and licked them happily in greeting. 'We have just time before it gets dark.'

'Time for what?' asked John.

'Ah – that would be telling!' She stopped the car at the park. 'Out everyone. And you, lazybones.' As she gave Ben a gentle push, the boys saw that the bandage had gone.

'Thought we would give him his first run in the park,' she said. 'Do us all good,' and off she strode, dog and boys trailing in her wake.

She went to the stream. Right to where IT happened. Right by the weir. She stopped. Mick felt his throat tighten. Here it comes. The telling off he had been waiting for for weeks.

'Looks different,' said Mrs Greer. 'Nearly all the leaves gone. Different from last time we were all here.' She paused. 'No car on the grass.' She laughed. Mick was puzzled. She had not gone mad yet. 'It's all right,' she carried on. 'Just thought we ought to re-visit the scene of the crime. It's all ended well and I don't want you two to worry any more.' Mick was relieved. She was a bit strange at times, Mrs Greer, but at other times she seemed to know what boys were thinking. 'Come on, let's play football.' With that she produced the ball out of her shopping bag and gave it a superb kick, right across the grass. Mick, John and Ben joined in until it was too dark to play any longer. What a great day! Ben was better. Mick was not in trouble! He could not imagine a better day.

Little did he know that there was another great, even better, day coming up. A day that would pass his wildest dreams. He did not even know that it was being planned.

His first inkling that something was in the air was one Friday evening in November. Mum had arrived to collect Mick and, as usual, she was nattering to John's mum.

'All set then?' she asked. 'Have they guessed?' Guessed what? thought Mick, listening through the door. One day he would get caught at it but until then it was the best way of finding out what was going on.

'Don't think so,' replied Mrs Greer. 'When are you telling Mick?'

'Well, I'll have to say something tonight or he'll never be up in time. Shush, I can hear them coming.'

Up in time for what? Mick was dying to ask.

Later, at home, Mick acted out the world's biggest yawn and stretched. If he went to bed early Mum would have to tell him what was going on.

'Bed for you,' said Mum, looking up from the flickering television screen. 'You've got a long day tomorrow.'

'Why?' asked Mick, trying to look surprised.

'Well, the Greers are going out for the day and they've said you can go,' replied Mum. 'I'm looking after Ben for the day. It's too far for him to travel.'

'Where are we going?' Mick jumped up.

'Ah – that would be telling.' And no matter how hard he pestered Mum she would not tell him. Neither would the Greers the next morning.

'Is it a fun-fair, or adventure park, or seaside, or . . .'

'Not Aunt Ethel's,' groaned John.

'Or the caravan,' laughed Mick.

'You'll see,' was all Mr Greer would say. Wherever it was, it was a long way. Miles of motorway and blurred countryside, over huge fly-overs, on and on. At last they stopped, but it was only a motorway service station. Mrs Greer shepherded them into the canteen.

'I said about two o'clock,' she said to her husband. 'We're doing okay for time.'

'Come on, Mum, tell us,' begged John. 'How much further? I'm bored stiff. It can't be that good.'

'Wait and see.' Mum winked mysteriously.

After egg, beans and chips, followed by sticky buns, they carried on with the journey. Mr Greer turned off the motorway into a grey dismal town. He and Mrs Greer had a friendly argument about her abilities as a map-reader. Well, lack of abilities. They came to the same roundabout at least three times.

'Here, swop places,' Mr Greer stopped and moved out of the driving seat. 'We'll never find 49 Malvern Avenue, at this rate.'

'49 Malvern Avenue?' chorused the boys in the back. That sounded dead boring. Hardly 'fun-world' was it?

Mick thought, I hope they are not visiting ancient relatives. I hate meeting new people who pat me on the head, and ask stupid questions about how old I am, or what I like at school. I wish I hadn't come.

'Is this it?' said John in disbelief as they pulled up outside a row of terrace houses. 'There's nothing here.'

'I'll just check it's the right one,' said Mrs Greer to her husband, ignoring John's grumbles. She disappeared up a garden path and into a house. After an age she came out, waving.

'Come on!' she called. 'This is it. Anita's.'

Anita's, thought Mick. Who on earth was Anita? He trailed slowly up the path, scuffing his feet on the loose gravel. As he went into the house with John he could hear the Greers laughing with this Anita-person. She had her back to him, but looked quite young, about Emma's age, with long blonde hair flowing down her back.

'I have put her in the kitchen,' she said quietly in answer to some question Mr Greer asked her. 'Now, all sit down and I will get a drink. Tea all right?'

'Yes, lovely, I am parched,' said Mrs Greer. Mick stared at his feet and just nodded his head.

'What about the boys? Tea?' Mick nodded again. Silly girl, couldn't she see him?

'Mick and John would like tea,' said Mr Greer. 'Mick's on the settee and John is by the fireplace.'

Anita turned and smiled at them but she seemed to be looking straight over Mick's head. He was not that bad to look at!

As Anita was leaving the room she stopped for a moment. 'Now?' she asked and Mr Greer replied that 'now' seemed a very good time. Anita shut the door and the four people sat silently in the room. Mrs Greer looked as if she was gasping to laugh out loud and there was even a twinkle in Mr Greer's eye.

The door opened and Anita came back in the room. But not alone. She was holding a white harness handle. And in the harness was a dog. A beautiful golden dog. A guide dog!

'Sandy,' screamed Mick, jumping to his feet. 'It's Sandy! John, it's Sandy!'

He dived across the room and flung his arms round her neck. Fortunately Anita had realized what might happen and let go of the harness.

'Oh, Sandy, Sandy.' Mick was so happy. John joined him and the two boys hugged the dog. Mick buried his face into the long hair on her neck. He tried as hard as he could but was unable to stop the tears. They dripped onto the silky coat but this time they were tears of happiness. Here she was, his beloved Sandy, she had not forgotten him. He could hear Anita and the Greers talking and laughing.

'Well, I knew he would be glad to see her but I never expected he would be this glad,' Mrs Greer kept on saying, like a record that had got stuck. Mick sat on the floor, very close to Sandy. He noticed, however, that she spent most of her time looking at Anita. He realized that she belonged to her now but it did not matter. Anita had 'got Sandy' and it felt okay.

14

The rest of the day flew by. Anita was nice. She seemed to like answering their questions about Sandy. And there were plenty of questions!

Anita told them how she had been waiting for a guide dog for a long time.

'You see,' she said, 'my eyes have always been bad and now I cannot see anything. I've just started at college here and I need Sandy to help me find my way about. When I lived at home, my parents took me everywhere but now I can do things for myself.'

'Is there just you and Sandy living here?' asked John.

'No, I've got a friend called Jackie who shares the house with me.'

'How does Sandy get you to college?' asked Mick. The Sandy he knew spent most of her time charging off in the opposite direction he wanted her to go in.

'I will show you, if you like,' offered Anita.

'I don't know,' said Mrs Greer. 'It's getting dark and Mick and John don't know their way around this town at all.'

'It's always dark for me,' said Anita quietly. Mick looked straight at her. It must be awful to be always dark. He shut his eyes tightly. Nothing. It would be like that for Anita. The strange thing was that she did not seem sad. In fact she was bouncy and happy.

'Oh, go on, Mum, don't be a spoil-sport,' begged John. 'We'll be all right.'

'It will take less than an hour to get there and back,' said Anita. 'I would love to show the boys what Sandy can do. If you want, you could stay here and have a rest. Jackie will be back soon.'

So off they went. It was amazing. Anita had to hold the harness. That was because she and Sandy had been trained together. Sandy obeyed her commands. She led her down the path through the gate and alongside the roadway. Then Sandy stopped and turned sharply and they went along an entry between the houses.

'How did she know where to turn? asked Mick.

'She's clever,' replied Anita. 'You wait until you see what else she can do.'

Sandy led them to a zebra crossing, waited and, when a car stopped, boldly marched across the road. She turned a couple of corners and came to rest at a bus-stop.

'This is where I catch the bus to college,' explained Anita. 'Do you want to try a bus-ride with us?'

'Oh, yes,' exclaimed the boys.

'Okay. Don't fuss Sandy so she can concentrate.'

When the bus came, Sandy climbed slowly up the steps, stopped to let Anita pay the driver, and led her to an empty seat.

'How did you know how to pay the driver?' asked John.

Anita spread her fingers out. 'The various coins feel different. Here, you try.' She took a handful of change out of her pocket and passed it to them. Mick felt the money. Okay, some felt different but he would never have managed to give the right change to the driver.

'Technical college,' called the driver. Without a word from Anita, Sandy got up and guided Anita to the doorway, the boys following on behind. As the door opened, they carefully went down the steps. Then Sandy led them to a subway, through it and up the ramp the other end. Eventually they stopped at a doorway in the middle of all the college buildings. Sandy sat down and sniffed at Anita's hand.

'She's not sure what is going on,' Anita said. 'The college is locked up because it's Saturday afternoon. Usually she would take me to the lift and up to the fifth floor. Then along the corridor to a lecture room. She sits at my feet when I'm working. Then at dinner-time we go to the canteen and later she brings me back again.'

'Does she take you anywhere else?' It was Mick's turn to ask.

'Oh, yes. The library, shopping – mind you a friend has to come with me then. One tin of food feels very much like another! She likes going to the butcher's. He nearly always gives her a bone. Last night she took me to a party.' Anita chuckled. 'I don't think she was very impressed with the music though.' She paused. 'Time for the return journey. Come on, you two,' and off she set.

On the way back to her home, Mick was very thoughtful. Anita could do more or less anything — except see. She could go where she wanted, when she wanted. He could hardly believe how fast she walked. He shut his eyes, after they got off the bus, and tried to walk. After a couple of shaky steps, he had to open them. It was much too scary to walk around with them shut. He would bump into something. Yet Anita had not bumped into anything. It was mind-blowing.

'Come on, slow-coach,' called Anita. Mick had not noticed that he was getting left behind. How did Anita know?

When they got back to the house, they met Jackie. She had got tea ready. Anita took Sandy's harness off and told her to stay in her basket. Sandy did! No trying to pinch bits of food, like when she was a puppy at the Greers'.

That was it, thought Mick. She was not a puppy. The Sandy he had loved had been an adorable rascal, a bundle of fun, to play with, to hug, to tell secrets to. This Sandy was different. She had grown up. She had greeted him but he knew she was Anita's dog. All the while that they ate tea, Sandy watched Anita's face.

'Why does Sandy look at you all the time?' asked Mick. 'She's doing it now.'

'Well, she wants to know if I need her to do something. If I got up and fetched her harness, she would come straight here. She knows that the harness means work. She's my eyes, you see.'

Mick did see. Well, a bit anyway. Anita was blind and Sandy did the looking for her.

Mick realized something with a start. Anita needed Sandy far more than he did. This was the right place for Sandy, not at home with him. Sandy belonged here. He remembered back to that awful day when Dad had come into his room, just after he had run away. He had told Mick that Sandy had gone. Mick remembered how he felt. Awful. Like dying. The pain of the memory shot inside him. He could not finish the slice of cherry cake in his hand. He had never said goodbye to Sandy. He got up and walked across to her basket. Everyone was too busy talking and eating to notice what he was doing. Mick crouched down by Sandy, put his mouth to her floppy ear and whispered.

'I've come to say goodbye, Sandy. You can go now. You're not mine. You are Anita's. That's okay. You be a good girl for Anita, won't you?' He sat down and silently stroked her. He felt strangely at peace. Seeing Sandy today had been marvellous. Somehow he could accept that she had gone. He knew she was in the right place.

The Greers were making signs of leaving.

'Just take a few photos,' said Mr Greer. He turned to Mick. 'I'll get you a copy, too. Put it with the one of Sandy as a pup.'

Anita obliged by putting on Sandy's harness. Mr Greer finished off his film, and Sandy was left in peace.

'Thanks so much,' said Mrs Greer. 'It's been lovely meeting you. We will keep in touch.'

'It's been a pleasure,' replied Anita. 'No trouble at all. I'm one of the lucky ones. I've got my "eyes" to look after me.'

'Lucky ones?' queried John.

'Oh, yes,' Anita sighed. 'Lots of people are waiting to get guide dogs.'

As they drove off on the long journey home, they all talked about the day until, feeling tired, they fell silent, lost in their own thoughts. Mick was re-living the past year. Was it only ten months ago that he had run away with Sandy? That Bod-place seemed like a different world. Maybe Steve was right after all. Perhaps wanting Sandy for himself was selfish. After all, if he had 'got Sandy', Anita could never have had her. And, however you looked at it, Anita needed Sandy far more than he did. So that was why God had not answered his prayer. God knew Anita needed Sandy the most. It was not because God was being mean and nasty to him. God was bothered about him, and other people too.

'Thank you, God, for Sandy,' he said in his head. 'Thank you she belongs to Anita now. Please look after them. Thanks too for helping me to work out what Steve was on about, you know, my prayer being selfish. I did not mean to be selfish. I am sorry for being mad at you when you did not give me Sandy.' He stopped. That had got that sorted out with God. Now God knew he was not cross at him. He could carry on talking to him about anything. Mind you, perhaps he had better stop telling God exactly how to answer his prayers!

Some other Tiger books which you might like to read . . . . .

Smugglers' Cove
Pat Coleman
Seb and Fiona are spending their summer holidays at their grandmother's house. They make friends with Mike and Peter and together go exploring the caves along the coast. Mike and Peter have heard stories of smugglers in bygone days and want to find the caves they used. After a frightening incident on the beach they discover that Peter has more than his fair share of problems and they determine to help him find a way round them.

The Fen Street Flyer
Graham Jones
Another amusing story about Paul, Oliver, Richard, Eddie and the other characters in *The Bike*. As a joke, Paul and Oliver are nominated to take part in a talent contest for a TV show. Their performance is a disaster but as a result the organisers discover the Fen Street Rock Calypso band and invite them on the show. Then their instruments are stolen just before the show. Paul decides to do some investigating, starting with Eddie.

The Inca Trail
Vivien Whitfield
A collection of stories about children in Peru whose lives are very different from ours. Roberto is a shepherd up in the mountains who wants to get away to the town. Lisbet lives in a shanty town and has never seen the sea

until she goes to camp. Luis is a guide to the tourists who come to visit the Inca ruins.

The Shell Box

Carol Oldham

It is the summer holidays and Laura and Tim are looking forward to a seaside holiday with their cousins, Mark and Alice. Then Theresa is fostered with Laura's family and Laura becomes very possessive of her, resenting Mark's attempts to be friendly to Theresa and imagining he is trying to get her away from Laura. When Theresa is lost one day, Mark gets the blame and he decides to make a shell box for Theresa to show he is sorry. Laura takes the box before he can give it to Theresa and hides it. Then things really start to go wrong